D1352326

The Dragon hadn't spoken a word since the day it had submitted to her, inside the prison-book. She'd never been able to pull its thread toward the world to summon or control it. It just sat there, deep in her mind, like a toad at the bottom of a pond.

Now she took hold of the thread. *Can you hear me?* she thought at it.

I can hear you, little sister.

A dozen questions came to mind. *Why haven't you spoken to me before now? Can Isaac hear you too?*

No. His mind is closed to me. And there was never a need before. But now you are in great danger.

Danger? She looked up at the castle. *Here?*

Yes. You are entering a labyrinth. If you continue, you are lost.

993768279 7

www.totallyrandombooks.co.uk

THE MAD APPRENTICE

Also available in The Forbidden Library series:

The Forbidden Library

THE MAD APPRENTICE

DJANGO WEXLER

VOLUME II IN THE FORBIDDEN LIBRARY

Illustrated by Alexander Jansson

CORGI BOOKS

THE MAD APPRENTICE
A CORGI BOOK 978 0 552 56868 5

First published in Great Britain by Corgi Books,
an imprint of Random House Children's Publishers UK
A Penguin Random House Company

Penguin
Random House
UK

This edition published 2015

1 3 5 7 9 10 8 6 4 2

Copyright © Django Wexler, 2015
Cover and interior illustrations copyright © Alexander Jansson, 2015
Cover type copyright © David Wyatt

The right of Django Wexler to be identified as the author of this work has been
asserted in accordance with the Copyright, Designs and Patents Act 1988.

All rights reserved. No part of this publication may be reproduced, stored in a
retrieval system, or transmitted in any form or by any means, electronic, mechanical,
photocopying, recording or otherwise, without the prior permission of the publishers.

Penguin Random House is committed to a sustainable future for our business, our readers
and our planet. This book is made from Forest Stewardship Council® certified paper.

MIX
Paper from
responsible sources
FSC® C016897
FSC
www.fsc.org

Set in Lomba

Corgi Books are published by Random House Children's Publishers UK,
61–63 Uxbridge Road, London W5 5SA

www.randomhousechildrens.co.uk
www.totallyrandombooks.co.uk
www.randomhouse.co.uk

Addresses for companies within The Random House Group Limited
can be found at: www.randomhouse.co.uk/offices.htm

THE RANDOM HOUSE GROUP Limited Reg. No. 954009

A CIP catalogue record for this book is available from the British Library.

Printed and bound by CPI Group (UK) Ltd, Croydon, CR0 4YY

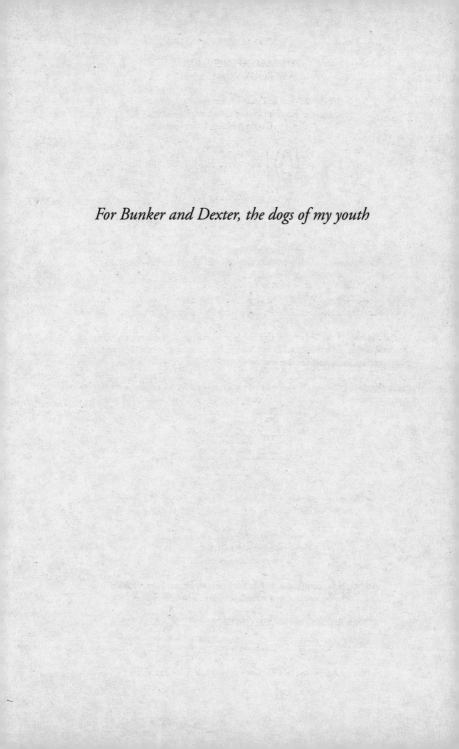

For Bunker and Dexter, the dogs of my youth

CONTENTS

CHAPTER ONE

THE SWAMP

THE SWAMP WAS HOT, moist, and silent. For a long time, nothing moved except groping tendrils of fog, playing over the muck and twisting between the hunchbacked trees. An occasional dragonfly skimmed through the reeds on crystalline wings. Overhead, the sun was fat and orange, motionless as if it had been nailed to the pale blue sky.

Then, in the distance, there was the sound of raised voices, and the rustle of someone moving through the underbrush. The dragonflies scattered. A moment later, one of the fogbanks quivered and disgorged a girl, picking her way with caution along a spit of what passed for solid ground.

She was twelve or thirteen, dressed in practical trousers and a leather vest, with her hair tied up to keep it out of the way. She was sweating freely, her pale, freckled cheeks already reddening in the sun, but her eyes were alert, scanning the trees and hollows around her.

Sitting on her shoulder was a small gray cat. His claws were fastened into her vest with desperate strength, as though he was terrified of falling off. Insofar as a cat can have an expression, this one looked very unhappy.

The girl and the cat were named Alice and Ashes-Drifting-Through-the-Dead-Cities-of-the-World (or Ashes, for short), respectively. When they reached the top of the hummock, Alice stopped and turned in a slow circle, while Ashes lashed his tail in an irritable sort of way. It was the cat who finally broke the awkward silence that had grown up between them.

"What," he said, "are we doing here?"

"We're looking for some kind of monster," Alice said. Her master, Geryon, had told her what it was called, some complicated Latin name, but she hadn't committed it to memory. "I've got to fight it. *You* know."

"I know why *you're* here. This seems like exactly the sort of place you *would* visit, all mucky water and mud and monsters. What I want to know is why *I* should have to be here. I'm half cat, after all. I should be above this sort of thing."

"*You* are here because you did your business in Master Geryon's slippers," Alice said. "Again."

"He has no proof of that," Ashes said, tail whipping against the back of her neck.

"There are hardly a lot of suspects," she said.

"Hmph," Ashes snorted.

"You should be glad Geryon didn't turn you into a toad."

"If he had to send me to babysit you," the cat said, "why did it have to be somewhere so . . . wet?"

"You should have seen the last place," Alice muttered. She wasn't sure she'd ever be able to get into a swimming pool again. "Now be quiet. I need to concentrate."

There was a rustle in the bushes, farther on, and a small creature emerged. It looked a bit like a wingless bird, with an oval body balanced on two clawed feet and a long, pointed beak. The sleek black coat that covered it was fur, though, and not feathers.

It was called a swarmer, and Alice knew that it was not, in fact, a separate creature at all, but only a part of a larger entity, like an ant or a bumblebee. The Swarm had been the first creature she'd bound, back when she'd known nothing of Readers or magic and she'd accidentally stumbled into a prison-book. The individual swarmers could be almost cute, but she couldn't quite forget the sound of hundreds of them running after her, claws *tiktiktik*ing on the stone floor as they *quirked* for blood.

Right now she was using a few of them to scout, since the creature that occupied *this* prison-book was not being terribly cooperative. She could, after much practice, peer through their eyes without letting her real body fall over, but she still wasn't good at dealing with more than one of them at once. It didn't help that they were poorly suited to the swamp—they were heavier than they looked, and every time one of them stepped into a puddle, it sank to the bottom like a stone and had to scramble to get out.

Alice herself was far from keen on the swamp, as a matter of fact. It was like the water and the land had gotten mixed up, somehow. Even the dry bits were covered in thick, sticky mud, and the innumerable channels and shallow ponds were covered with floating weeds that made them look just like land until she put her foot in them and muddy water poured into her boot. To top things off, the mosquitoes were eating her alive, and her sunburned skin stung whenever she squashed one.

She checked her swarmers, one by one, but all they could really see were more weeds, a disadvantage of being only a foot high. *This isn't working.* She sighed and let them pop out of existence.

At least now I can do something about the mosquitoes. At the back of her mind were the threads of magic that led to her bound creatures. A silver thread for the Swarm, a deep nut-brown one for the tree-sprite, and a deep blue one for her latest acquisition: a big, toothy creature Geryon had called a devilfish, which could let her glow in the dark or breathe underwater.

Beneath them all, at the very edge of her mental reach, a final thread coiled in rings of darkest obsidian. That one led to the Dragon, which had remained stubbornly impervious to her every attempt to summon or command it.

Alice mentally wrapped the Swarm thread around herself, giving her skin the tough, rubbery resilience of the little creatures. *The next bug that tries to take a bite out of me is going to be very surprised.* Then she opened her eyes and stared around the fetid, baking swamp, frowning.

"This isn't right," she said. "The creature isn't supposed to *hide*. In every other prison-book the thing was champing at the bit for a fight."

"Perhaps this one's shy," Ashes said. "Or perhaps I shouldn't have come with you. It may be deterred by my magnificent presence. I am very intimidating, after all." He yawned. "Yes, that's probably it. Why don't you leave me in that tree, and you can get on with things while I have a nice little lap?"

Alice rolled her eyes. "Can't you . . . sniff it out or something?"

The cat's fur bristled. "I think you may have mistaken me for some sort of *hound*."

"Don't be silly," Alice said. She put on a sly smile. "I just figured that whatever a stupid *dog* could do, you'd be able to do better. Being half cat, and all."

"I can see what you're trying to do, and it won't work," Ashes said. "Don't think you can bait me."

"Fair enough, fair enough. I've been thinking of asking Geryon if I could have a puppy anyway."

"A puppy?" Ashes sputtered.

"A golden retriever, maybe. You two would look so cute together. I can just see him licking your face with his big slobbery tongue—"

"All right, all *right*," Ashes said. "You don't have to get gruesome."

"Then you can smell something?"

"In this muck? Not a chance." His whiskers twitched, and he shut his eyes. "If you'll be quiet for a moment, though, I may be able to *hear* something. We half-cats have excellent ears." One eye cracked, just slightly, so he could glare at her. "Much better than any *canine*."

Alice suppressed a giggle, and stood in silence while Ashes' ears twitched and pivoted, like tiny searchlights. Eventually he raised a paw and pointed.

"I don't know if it's what we're looking for," he said, "but I can hear something big breathing, over in that direction."

"That's probably it," Alice said. "These prison-books never seem to have much life beyond the prisoner." Though why this one included *mosquitoes* was beyond Alice. She started down the hillock in the direction Ashes indicated, probing ahead of her with the toe of her boot to make sure of her footing. The mud sucked at her feet with every step, but fortunately Geryon had provided her with a pair of very fine leather boots; her ordinary shoes would have been lost to the mire long ago.

She came to a stream, a channel of deeper, fast-running water moving through the muck, and hopped across it on a pair of convenient rocks. Ahead, the plants grew taller and closer together, forming an impenetrable thicket. Alice glanced at Ashes, and he nodded in that direction.

"I don't see anything," she said.

"It's in there somewhere."

"Are you sure?"

The cat only sniffed haughtily. Alice sighed and pulled the Swarm thread a little tighter around herself for protection, then crept forward.

There *was* something in there, deep inside the curling branches. A solid dark mass, like a hump of stone. But it was watching her. She edged sideways, and saw the shape move, a fraction of a degree.

"I see it," Alice said. "Hold on."

Ashes didn't bother to answer, but his claws were tiny pinpricks against her skin, even through the vest. Alice took another step forward, and another, then halted when the half-hidden creature shifted. It gave a low *chuff*, like a car engine starting up.

Then, all at once, it exploded into motion. Alice hadn't expected it to be so *fast*—it crashed out of the thicket in a blur of frantic motion. She got the sense of something gray and compact, with legs working frantically and wicked, pointed horns aimed directly at her.

The Alice of a year ago would have panicked. She'd only read about ferocious creatures in books or seen them at the zoo, safely behind bars. But that Alice no longer existed. *This* Alice was a year older and had spent the last six months as a Reader's apprentice. In that capacity she'd been squashed, drowned, frozen, and otherwise nearly killed more times than she could count, and it took considerably more than a charging monster to faze her.

None of this meant that she was *stupid*, however, and she threw herself to one side at the last moment, giving the thing no time to adjust its path. The creature took quite a while to slow down once it realized it had missed, skidding through the mud and sending up a wave of dirt and pebbles as it slewed to a halt.

It was, she saw, now that she got a good look at it, a dinosaur. Not a terribly large one, certainly—its shoulders were a bit higher than Alice's head, which put its eyes just about level with hers. It had a lumpy, pebble-skinned body and four stumpy, powerful legs, with broad flat feet like an elephant's. A short tail whipped back and forth, like an excited dog's. Most notable, though, was the massive crest running back from its head, from which sprouted four long, curving horns that stretched out past its beady black eyes and bird-like beak. Most of it was a dark gray, but the horns faded to pure white at the ends, and the tips looked very sharp.

One foot pawed the ground, which put Alice in mind of a bull, getting ready to charge. She got to her feet, slowly, brushing chunks of mud from her trousers.

"Okay," she said. "Now we know what we're dealing with. Are you all right?"

There was a silence. Alice felt the distinct absence of weight from her shoulder.

"Ashes?" She kept her eyes glued to the dinosaur's, waiting for it to make a move. "Where are you?"

"Here," came the cat's voice, a bit higher than normal.

"Where?"

"*Here.*"

Alice finally spotted him. One of the lumps on the creature's pebbled gray skin moved, revealing itself to be a small gray cat hanging on for dear life. All his fur was standing on end, and his tail stuck straight up like a flag.

"How did you get *there*?"

"I'm not exactly sure," Ashes said. "I thought you might get clobbered, so I abandoned ship, so to speak, and grabbed the first thing I could get a hold of."

"Your faith in me is astounding," Alice said.

"I thought perhaps getting clobbered was part of your plan," Ashes said. "You always come up with the cleverest plans. Now will you please *get me down from here*?"

Alice took a step to the left, and the dinosaur turned to face her, still pawing the ground. She could see its hindquarters tensing as it prepared to charge.

"That . . . may be a bit difficult," she said. "Can't you jump?"

"I would really rather not."

"In that case, hang on tight."

"*Always* the cleverest plans—"

The dinosaur charged. Ashes' rear legs lost their grip and he scrambled madly to stay on top, his claws making no impression at all on the creature's thick hide. Alice guessed the needle beaks of the Swarm would have a similar lack of effect, so she kept that thread tightly wound around her. She jumped aside again, like a bullfighter, letting the creature sweep past her and into the long, tangled branches of one of the reedy swamp trees.

Before it could turn, Alice yanked on the tree-sprite thread in her mind and grabbed a branch, extending her power through it and into the main body of the tree. It was a thin, unhappy plant, eking out a bare existence in the drowned soil and constant fog, but it responded to the tree-sprite's magic and came alive under Alice's hand. The long, wispy branches snapped out and lashed themselves around the dinosaur, wrapping its thick body in green. She guided them around Ashes, who had maintained his perch by virtue of sinking his fangs into the back of the creature's neck.

The dinosaur struggled, tossing its head and snapping branches with its horns, but more and more limbs cocooned it as the tree bent forward like a vegetable spider. It gave a frustrated roar and turned, laboriously, toward Alice. The thing's strength was incredible; even the little swamp tree could have torn the arms and legs off an ordinary human, but the dinosaur fought its way forward inch by inch. It pulled the branches as far as they could go, straining like a dog at the leash, beak snapping. Alice almost felt sorry for it, trying so hard and getting . . . *nowhere* . . .

There was a *crack*, and the dinosaur inched a foot

forward. Another branch tore with a wet *snap,* then two more. Ashes, who had been cautiously examining the possibility of making a jump to the ground, leaped back and grabbed on with all four legs. Alice moved away as far as she could while maintaining her focus on the tree, throwing all her power into pulling the dinosaur down.

But it was tearing free. No matter how tight she held on, the endurance of the little dinosaur seemed endless. One by one, and then in bunches, the fronds gave up the unequal struggle and tore. When half of them were gone, the trunk of the swamp tree, as thick as Alice's thigh, started to bend. Then, all at once, it broke in half with a *crack* like a gunshot, and the creature was free.

"Time for another plan, I think!" Ashes shouted.

The dinosaur shook the ragged ends of the tree branches off itself and glared at Alice with small, dark eyes. Alice stared back at it for a moment, then turned and ran.

"What are you doing?" Ashes shouted.

"Thinking!" Alice shouted back.

"Think faster!"

Branches whipped at her face, but her Swarm-toughened skin kept her from feeling the impacts. She was more concerned about tripping on the slippery, muddy ground. The dinosaur was pounding along behind her, and rubber skin wouldn't help if it got her with those horns.

In a straightaway, the race would have been no contest. In spite of its stubby legs, the horned monster's tremendous strength could generate a considerable turn of speed, and if it was getting tired at all, it didn't show. Alice was already winded, and she only stayed ahead by ducking and dodging around bushes and past tree trunks, leaping lightly over narrow puddles and splashing through larger ones. The dinosaur skidded back and forth in her wake like a car trying to drive on a sheet of ice, legs kicking up sprays of goopy mud.

Think faster. She might be able to grow a tree to the size and thickness it would need to capture the thing, but that would take time she didn't have. *Besides, Ashes might get hurt. I need something quicker—*

The sound of running water came from ahead of her. It was the stream she'd crossed earlier, a clear, deep channel amidst the brackish standing water of the swamp. At the sight of it, she put her head down and summoned a burst of speed, breaking between a couple of trees with the dinosaur still right on her tail.

When she reached the bank, Alice jumped, aiming for

a nice big pool created by a fallen log and hoping desperately she wasn't about to break her leg against a rock. She hit the water with a mighty splash, the sound of which almost drowned out Ashes' plaintive cries.

"Oh, no. No, no, no, I don't like this plan, think harder, Aliiiiiice—"

Then she was underwater. The stream was as warm as bathwater, and tasted faintly of sulfur and dirt. The pool was only just deeper than Alice was tall, and swimming in all her clothes was harder than she'd expected. She fought through the clanging dimness, waiting—

The dinosaur followed her in, only moments later. She wasn't sure if it had wanted to or not, but it had been moving far too quickly to stop itself on the muddy ground, so it had ended up in the stream whatever its intention. It thrashed and wriggled, only a few feet away from her, surrounded by a froth of white water and bubbles.

The very first time Alice had ever fought a creature, she'd managed to trap it in deep water until it drowned. It was immediately obvious, though, that this was not going to be an exact reprise of that victory. The dinosaur righted itself quickly, and unlike the swarmers, it could swim, if only in a clumsy dog paddle. The water wasn't deep enough or wide enough for Alice to hide for long.

Fortunately, Alice had no intention of hiding. She had acquired a few tricks since that first night, and now she reached for the deep blue thread that led to the last creature she'd conquered. Letting the Swarm thread go, she wrapped the devilfish thread around herself, over and over until its power flooded through her body and she began to change.

There was a nauseating moment of *fluidity* between forms, but then her new body settled into place. She'd become an enormous, vicious-looking fish with a broad, fan-shaped tail and hundreds of tiny needle-sharp teeth. Patches of scales on her flanks glowed, turning the pool into a weird, flickering nightmare of shadow and unearthly green radiance, but the dinosaur was easily visible as it paddled toward shore. With a flick of her tail, Alice-the-fish surged forward, her jaw opening wide.

The dinosaur heard her coming, and lowered its horns in her direction, but in this form Alice was far more agile in the water. She darted easily around the clumsy thing and went for its shoulder, farther back than it could twist its head to snap at her. The strength in the devilfish's jaw was immense, and it felt like the easiest thing in the world to drive those hundreds of teeth through tough, scaly skin and into muscle. Blood filled Alice's mouth;

had she still been a girl, she would have gagged, but to the fish, the taste was heavenly.

Instead of ripping and tearing, as a real fish might have, Alice *pulled.* The dinosaur was a clumsy swimmer, and though it thrashed its legs, it was unable to resist being drawn back and *down* into the center of the pool until its head was completely underwater. Once she had it there, there was nothing to do but wait for it to give in. The creature's struggles became increasingly frantic, but Alice felt nothing but comfortable, warm water sluicing easily through her gills.

Submit, she thought at the dinosaur, extending her will. *Submit.* She could escape the prison-book by killing the prisoner, but she didn't like to do that if she didn't have to, even if it was only a dumb animal. Even the stupidest creatures, she'd found, could understand the concept of dominance.

Eventually, the dinosaur got the message. She could feel its resistance collapse, the essence of its spirit twining out into a thread that would be forever linked to her. As it did, the world began to fade away as the magic of the prison-book recognized that she'd accomplished her task and sent her back to where she'd come from.

When reality snapped back, for a horrible moment

she was drowning, choking, flopping wildly in a strange, alien environment. Hurriedly, she unwrapped the devil-fish thread. A moment later, she was a girl again, lying on her back and gasping for breath, dripping muddy water onto Geryon's study rug.

Chapter Two

THE WAY FORWARD

WELL DONE," SAID GERYON. He was at his desk, writing something, and he didn't look up.

It took Alice a moment to gather enough breath to sit up. Being a fish left her feeling a bit wobbly, and she had to concentrate to remember how her hands and feet worked. By the time she'd gotten a hold of herself, Geryon had laid his pen carefully aside and turned around.

"Are you all right?" His voice was devoid of sympathy. As ever, Geryon could have passed for a jolly old grandpa—shabby, ink-stained clothes, flyaway gray hair and wild, bushy sideburns—except for his eyes. They were dark, exacting, and intelligent, forever the eyes of a master sitting in judgment. Geryon had helped Alice—saved her, really, from the fairy Vespidian and the other agents of the old Readers who wanted to kidnap her—but when she met his gaze, it reminded her that he was not in any sense her friend.

"I'm fine, sir," Alice said. "Just winded." She looked around. "Ashes? Are you okay?"

There was no answer, and Alice had a moment of worry. Ashes had probably gone into the stream along with the dinosaur, but she hadn't seen him when she'd dragged the creature under. *He must have gotten away. Cats can swim, right?*

Then she heard a long, low, growl, and sighted a dark shape huddled under one of the leather armchairs. Alice bent to peer beneath it, and a paw swiped out, nearly catching her on the nose.

"Alice!" Ashes spat, furious. "How is it every time we go on one of these expeditions *I* end up getting *wet*? You're doing it on purpose!"

"Nothing else occurred to me at the time," Alice said. "It's not like I didn't get soaked too."

"It's different for you fur-less apes!" Ashes squirmed out from under the chair. Alice had to admit he made for a pathetic sight, his sodden fur clumped in tufts and his tail still dripping. He began furiously licking one paw. "Blech! I'll be tasting mud for a week!"

"I'm sorry," Alice said.

"No you're not. You're already thinking how you can dunk me again!"

Ashes shook himself and stalked out the door. It is impossible for a soaked cat to stalk with any degree of dignity, but Alice held her chuckle until he was gone. Even Geryon's face was touched with a fleeting smile.

"I think your punishment was effective, sir," Alice said. "Although it might have been a bit harsh."

"Chastising Ashes was a secondary concern," Geryon said. "There will always be times when you must worry about defending others, in addition to yourself. I thought the experience would prove valuable."

Alice swallowed and nodded. "Yes, sir."

"You have the creature's thread?"

"Yes, sir." Alice could feel it, a twisting cord the color of yellowed ivory, at the back of her mind with the others.

"Can you summon its power?"

She was tired from the fight, but Alice took hold of the dinosaur's thread and wrapped it around herself. It required considerable strength.

"Yes, sir."

"Excellent. How do you feel?"

Looking down at herself, Alice could see nothing obvious had changed. She raised her hand, then took a cautious step.

"As though I were almost weightless, sir."

"It is your strength that has increased. Try lifting the chair."

She took hold of the armchair, a heavy wood-and-leather thing that looked like it dated from the previous century. Ordinarily, just pushing it across the floor would have been hard, but she was delighted to find that it came easily off the ground in her grip, as though it were made of straw. It creaked as she held it over her head in one hand, shedding dust everywhere.

"Very good," Geryon said. "The enhancements of the body are crude tricks, but essential. A Reader should never be balked in a task by mere physical barriers. Let the thread go."

"Yes, sir." Alice put the chair down and let the dinosaur's power slip away. She felt as though she'd suddenly put on a lead coat.

"A word of warning. Lifting things is all well and good, but running and jumping with amplified strength take a bit of practice. I encourage you to experiment, but do so carefully."

Alice wondered how high she could jump, with the dinosaur's power coiled in her legs, and resolved to try it at the first opportunity. *If I have something soft to land on.* "Yes, sir."

"That will be all. You may have the rest of the day free."

"Thank you, sir."

Geryon waved her away, already turning back to his writing. Alice left the study, still dripping muddy water, and headed straight for the bath. Ashes was right—there were definitely advantages to being human, and not having to *lick* herself clean was one of them.

It had been six months since Mr. Black, Geryon's right-hand man, had picked her up at the train station in his ancient Model T. She'd arrived at the Library alone in a world that had started fraying dangerously at the edges. She'd gotten hold of a loose thread, that night she'd first seen Vespidian threatening her father. When she'd given it a tug, to her surprise and horror, the whole fabric of normality had crumbled to bits like rotten cloth. Underneath was . . . something else.

She'd started working in the endless magical library, guarded by a giant black cat who seemed to be made out of shadows. She'd learned to do magic, and she'd nearly died, twice. It was amazing how anything—even the Library, with its talking cats and invisible servants— could become routine. Even when your whole world had come to pieces, eventually it all came down to what you had to get done today before bedtime, and tomorrow, and the next day.

Every morning now, she had a brief chat with her master, and he would set the day's task for her. Sometimes it was basic work: gathering scraps of magic from the books for Mr. Wurms or fetching and carrying things the scholar needed. Other times, Geryon would interest himself in her training, watching her practice with her summoned creatures or showing her some trick. Alice got the sense she was doing well in this regard; Geryon seemed pleased, at least, and she had no other yardstick by which to gauge her progress.

More rarely, the old Reader would send her on what he called "errands," through one of the many portal-books in the wild back reaches of the library. For the most part these involved picking up or dropping off packages. Alice had gotten the sense, talking to Ashes, that there was a kind of highly paranoid economy among the old Readers. They would agree to trade one book or artifact for another, but the actual exchange couldn't be done in any of their libraries, since no Reader would risk visiting another in the seat of his power. It had to be done on neutral ground, somewhere out in one of the book-worlds. Other times, Geryon would send her just to look at something, and report back what she had found. She was never sure which of these tasks were things he really needed, and which were simply tests, so she applied herself diligently to all of them.

As a result, she had now been to more worlds than she could easily count. Some of them were ordinary, with forests and hills and grasslands, with only an extra moon or strange stars overhead to show her that she wasn't on Earth somewhere. Others were strange—blasted expanses of black rock, a forest of trees carved from marble, down to the smallest detail, a world of solid clouds and great, arching vines connecting them.

Alice was still determined to discover what had really happened to her father, but with no obvious leads to pursue, she'd had to make a longer-term plan. His disappearance had to be tied in with the world of the Readers, somehow, and so she threw herself into learning everything she could of their strange society and the powers they wielded. It was the sort of plan he would have approved of: When you aren't sure what to do, you ought to gather as much information as you can.

She wondered, though, if he would have approved of her work with Geryon. She wasn't sure *she* approved of it. Going into prison-books to force the creatures inside to submit to her—or killing them if they refused—still felt wrong somehow, though since her moment of defiance in the world of the tree-sprite, Geryon had not tested her against anything remotely intelligent or human-looking. "He is a Reader," Ending had said of Geryon. "His magic is based on cruelty and death." She half suspected her father would agree.

But this is the way forward. Emma, Geryon's mindless, obedient maidservant with her vacant eyes, was always there to remind Alice of the only other way out.

She hadn't had an afternoon off in a while. She thought about trying to catch up on her reading—there was a small and rather eclectic collection of books she'd borrowed from the library on her desk—but the sight of the sun pouring through her window changed her mind. She shrugged into a light jacket and went downstairs.

Pittsburgh's summer had been hot but brief, and now, at the end of October, fall was well enough along that it wasn't unusual to find frost on her windowpane in the morning. Now and again, though, the forces of the departing season seemed to rally for a last effort, and you got days like this one, with perfect golden autumn afternoons, just chilly enough to put red in your cheeks. A line of clouds darkened the sky to the west, suggesting the break in the weather wouldn't last, but for now it felt just right.

Alice wandered across the lawn that separated the Library mansion from the library building proper, which seemed like a good enough place to practice. She grabbed the dinosaur's thread and pulled it toward her, testing how much strain it put on her mental grip. More, she decided, than any of the creatures she had bound so far, but to her surprise it was well within the limits of her strength. Geryon had said her power would grow with practice, but this was the first time she'd realized it was actually happening.

The dinosaur appeared beside her and made a noise

that was half rumble and half honk, like a goose with a sore throat. Alice walked around it, giving it a leisurely inspection like a field marshal looking over his troops, then sent it walking toward the trees. Like most of the creatures she met, it was considerably more appealing when it wasn't trying to kill her. In spite of its size— Alice thought she might be able to *ride* it, although probably not for long—it had an endearingly doglike quality about it.

Spike, Alice decided. *I think I will call him Spike.* Though, for all she knew, Spike was a girl; she had no idea how one could tell, with dinosaurs.

She sent him rushing about, short tail swishing, getting a feel for how fast he could move and turn. Then, with a bit of hesitation, she turned him loose, ordering him to charge straight at the trunk of a great old oak on the other side of the clearing.

The results were spectacular. Spike's stubby legs got him up to full speed surprisingly quickly, and he lowered his head with its four horns and bony crest just before impact, slamming against the wood with an explosion of splinters and torn bark. Spike bounced back a foot and shook his head, slightly dazed from the blow, but the tree gave a tremendous *crack* and split where the dinosaur had struck it. The crown of the oak tipped sideways to lean drunkenly against its neighbor and the canopy shuffled and shed a torrent of yellow and brown leaves.

"I'm not sure Master Geryon would appreciate you destroying the foliage," said Ashes.

Alice looked around until she found him, lying on his back on a thick tree branch at the edge of the forest, soaking up the setting sun and looking at her, upside down.

"I needed some room to practice," Alice said. Plus, though she'd never say it aloud, these days sometimes she just wanted to break something. She let Spike vanish with a loud *pop* and reached for the tree-sprite thread. "Besides, I can fix it."

"It's so hard to resist playing with a new toy."

Alice glared at him, a little embarrassed, because that was exactly what she *had* been doing. She didn't like to think of her creatures that way, though. Her father had always taught her that living creatures were to be respected, and they weren't toys. *They're more like . . . pets.*

But she didn't know how to explain that to what was, after all, a cat, so she just walked over to the broken tree and put her hand on the trunk. The tree-sprite's power flowed through it, animating the splintered fibers and knitting them back together, and with a great creaking and groaning, the top half of the oak lifted back in position. More leaves fell, spiraling madly to the ground.

"Are you still angry at me, then?" she said to Ashes, when the tree was repaired.

He blinked, and rolled onto his stomach, wiping at his ear with one paw. "Nah. Too much work, and it's too nice a day." The cat yawned. "Just don't do it again."

"I'll do my best," Alice said.

Ashes looked around with exaggerated caution, and lowered his voice. "By the way, Mother said you should come by tomorrow and see the acorns."

Alice blinked, and matched his quiet tone. "Why? Has it worked this time?"

"She didn't tell *me*. Come and see, she said."

That sounded like Ending, all right. The great shadow-cat never said or did something simple if there was a way to make it obscure and complicated. That went hand in hand with being the guardian of a forbidden library, Alice supposed, but it made her frustrating.

Her secrecy also made Alice's relationship with her

master more complicated. As far as Geryon knew, Ending barely talked to Alice; in fact, the black cat often appeared when she was deep in the library on some task, and helped her practice aspects of her magic that Geryon had neglected. Just *why* Ending did this, Alice had no idea, but after the help Ending had offered trapping Vespidian, she didn't feel in a position to refuse.

The other thing Alice had never told Geryon about was Isaac, the other apprentice who'd broken in to the Library, and the way the two of them had worked together to bind the Dragon. Officially, she was still angry with Isaac for the trick he'd played on her, making her think he'd wanted to kiss her when he was only stealing the Dragon book for himself. But she found herself wishing sometimes that he would turn up, so she could be angry with him in person. At night, she found herself reaching out for the Dragon's thread, black and imperturbable as stone. Every so often she could feel the faintest of vibrations through it, and she knew that somewhere, in some world, Isaac was reaching out too.

The sun was slipping behind the trees, and this line of thought made her melancholy. Alice bid Ashes good-bye and went back up to the house to eat the dinner the invisible servants set for her. It was delicious, as always, but she found she barely tasted it. Her thoughts kept drifting back to her father, and what he would think of what she had become. When she was full, she went upstairs and tried to shake the feeling with a solid dose of last-century German philosophy, always guaranteed to produce a good night's sleep.

Once she was asleep, though, she dreamed.

Chapter Three
CENTRAL PARK

It was a perfect autumn afternoon, the air just chilly enough to put a little color in Alice's cheeks, but drenched in golden sunlight that made her feel deliciously warm and sleepy. She lay on a blanket beside the demolished remains of a picnic lunch. Her father sat next to her, his back propped against a tree stump, with his hands behind his head and his hat tipped down over his eyes.

Nobody went to Central Park anymore, or so the common wisdom ran. It was, Alice had to admit, a bit of a dump. Many of the trees were dead, the flowerbeds trampled, and the old wrought-iron benches overturned, lying legs-up like helpless turtles. Bits of trash were everywhere, and torn newspapers fluttered through the air when the wind blew, like tumbleweeds in a Western.

But Alice's father had been coming here for picnic lunches since he'd been a boy accompanying *his* father, and Alice loved the park because her father loved it. He knew all the best spots too, places off the usual paths, where a few trees were still clad in gorgeous red and gold and you could bask in the afternoon sun. A hundred yards away, a fluffy white sheep wandered, looking lost but contented, poking curiously at bits of garbage and tugging at the browning grass.

"Not supposed to be sheep here," Alice's father commented, to no one in particular. "The sheep are down at Sixty-fifth Street." He patted Alice on the shoulder, as though to reassure her. "I imagine someone will be along to collect it presently."

Alice yawned and closed her eyes. She could feel the prickle of the grass through the blanket, and hear the leaves rustling as the wind tugged them one by one from the trees. The sun was warm and soft on her face.

Whenever they came to the park, her father liked to talk to her about whatever was on his mind. Usually that meant business. He would tell her about pools and syndicates and high-leverage investment trusts, the prospects of US Steel and the Shenandoah Corporation. Alice understood most of it only dimly, but she didn't mind. What mattered was that he spoke to her as someone who was every bit as smart and grown-up as he was; in Alice's world of tutors and condescending servants, that was a treasure beyond price.

He'd started out talking about business today, but after a while he'd gone silent. Now, in a quiet voice, he said, "You don't remember Dad, do you?"

Alice shook her head.

"You were only two when he died," her father said. "It's a shame. He would have really liked you. I can see a lot of him in you."

Alice opened one eye and turned to look up at him. "Really?"

"Mmm-hmm. He was a smart man. Very logical." Her father cocked his head and grinned. "And stubborn. 'Never give up,' he would say. Whenever I complained about anything, that I was tired or it was too hard, he just shook his head and said, 'Never give up. Not ever.' It used to make me very angry with him, when I was your age."

Alice had a hard time imagining her father as a boy her age. It was hard to imagine him as anything but what he *was*, the solid, dependable rock around which her life

revolved. It was like wondering what the sun was like, before it was the sun.

"He would have been proud of you," her father said. He looked out over the park, past the wandering sheep, and sighed.

Something was wrong. Alice could feel it, feel some emotion in her father that she couldn't quite identify, but she didn't know what to do. She rolled over and pressed herself against his side, and his hand came down to tangle in her hair.

"You don't remember your mother either," he said, so quietly she wasn't sure he meant her to hear. "But I do. I *remember*." His voice was sad, but also fierce, full of quiet determination. "Someday . . ."

All Alice could do was hug him a little tighter. He tipped his hat down farther, to shade his eyes, and they sat there in silence until the sun touched the buildings on the West Side and the cold of the breeze began to bite. Then they went home and had chicken pot pies for dinner. They were her father's favorite, and she loved them because he loved them.

Alice woke up and thought it was before dawn, judging by the gray, dead light, but when she looked outside, she found the sky covered by clouds from edge to edge. A spattery, fitful rain *pinked* and *tinked* against the glass. The sun was nowhere to be seen.

She cleaned up and dressed slowly, still half mired in the dream. She hadn't thought about that day for a long time. Her life *before* had faded into the background, somehow, of her daily life at the Library. It was why she was here, but she couldn't think about it without feeling awful, like there was a horrible *gap* in her chest where her heart ought to have been. So, mostly, she didn't.

A wave of guilt descended on her like a bucket of cold water. *It's only been six months since he disappeared, and you're forgetting him already.* She closed her eyes, welcoming the painful thoughts as a sort of penance.

Emma brought her breakfast on a tray and Alice took it into her room, careful to remind the girl to go back to the kitchen afterward. Alice had learned long ago to be extremely literal when giving Emma directions; once, when she'd said "Here, take these," she'd returned hours later to find the maidservant still standing patiently with a tray in her arms. The food was excellent, as usual, but Alice raced through it and barely tasted a thing. She left the dirty dishes for the Library's invisible servants to clean up and hurried downstairs.

Geryon was waiting for her in his study, as usual. He was reading something, and Alice thought he looked troubled, but his face smoothed into a friendly mask as soon as he looked up at her.

"Good morning, Alice."

"Good morning, sir."

"Are you recovered from your trial yesterday?"

"Yes, sir."

"Excellent." Geryon tapped his chin thoughtfully. "You'll be in the library with Mr. Wurms today, at least for now." His eyes flicked to his desk and the papers there. "I may have something for you to take care of later on."

"Yes, sir." Alice hesitated. Geryon didn't like it when she asked too many questions, but the guilt churning in her gut wouldn't be assuaged unless she did *something*. "I wanted to . . . ask you something. Sir."

Geryon's expression was impassive, but his hard eyes fastened onto hers and didn't let go.

"Oh?" he said, after a moment of pointed silence.

"It's . . ." She paused, then spoke in a rush. "It's about my father."

"I see," Geryon said.

"It's just that you said you would look into what happened to him, to find out for certain. I know his ship went down, but we don't know why, or whether he was really on it." He promised that, after the Dragon incident. "And I've been here six months, and . . . I wondered, I mean if you'd . . . learned anything."

Another, longer silence. Geryon shook his head. His expression was compassionate, but it didn't touch his eyes, which were dark and hard as tiny marbles.

"I have put inquiries in motion, as we agreed," he said, "both for your sake, and to discover how the other Readers learned of your existence in spite of my protection."

Alice swallowed. She knew at least part of the answer to that last question—Mr. Black had betrayed her to Vespidian and his master, Esau-of-the-Waters. But that wasn't the whole story; Geryon had said there were other old Readers after her as well. Esau had wanted her badly enough to send Vespidian to the Library after her, but she had no idea if he'd also been involved in her father's disappearance. Nor, for that matter, did she know *why* she was so important to the old Readers, except that apprentices were hard to come by. *But that can't be all.*

At any rate, she'd promised not to tell Geryon about Mr. Black, in exchange for the traitorous servant's cooperation in trapping Vespidian so that Alice could interrogate him. *And because if Geryon found out, he'd have*

Mr. Black killed. Mr. Black had betrayed and hurt her, but Alice wasn't sure she was ready to condemn him to death with a word.

"That a Reader was involved is certain," Geryon went on. "But beyond that, I can't yet say. We are a jealous fraternity, and information is hard to come by. Still, I have . . . called in some favors, and set the wheels in motion." He put on a sad smile. "We will know the truth in the end, I promise you."

"Thank you." Alice bowed her head. She wanted to question him, but she felt as though she'd pushed her luck already. "I'll . . . go and help Mr. Wurms, then."

He waved a hand in dismissal. "I'll send for you if I have need."

The wind went from pleasantly cool to vicious, and sheets of rain swept across the lawn between the house and the library like the ranks of a conquering army. The change in weather matched her mood, which had turned dark after she'd nerved herself up to question Geryon and been put off with vague promises. *There has to be something he can do, something he knows.* The more she learned about magic, the more certain she'd become that her father had to be alive, somehow, taken by one of the old Readers to who knew what hidden fortress. She needed to *do* something, but she didn't know where to start.

There was an umbrella in her room, somewhere, but Alice couldn't be bothered to go and search for it. *I wonder if there's a creature I could bind that could keep me dry?* She checked the thought at once. That was old Reader thinking, the tendency to view the wondrous creatures that lived beyond the book-portals solely in terms of what power they could provide. For all that she was Geryon's apprentice, she didn't want to become that sort of person.

She made a dash for it, and the carved bronze door came open at her touch. She stepped into the warm, stuffy darkness of the anteroom and shook herself like a dog, spraying water against the stone.

The shelves were full of hurricane lamps, but she let them be. Now that she was a Reader, Alice didn't need them. She wrapped the devilfish thread loosely around her, and her hand began to glow an eerie blue green. She concentrated until it brightened enough for her to see by. As usual, at least a dozen cats had come to greet her at the inner door, eyes glowing otherworldly colors in the strange light. Alice waved politely, in case any of them could talk. None of the cats had ever spoken to her except

Ashes and Ending, but it didn't pay to make assumptions.

Beyond the cats, the regular grid of library shelves stretched out into infinity under the great dome with its obsidian markers. Alice set out down one of the aisles, trailing a cloud of disturbed dust. She didn't pay much attention to where she was going. One of the lessons she'd learned in the past six months was that landmarks and directions inside the library meant very little; you generally ended up where Ending wanted you to, no matter what direction you walked in.

This morning, that meant checking on the acorns before reporting for duty to Mr. Wurms. Alice was not surprised to find herself quickly leaving the tame, organized shelves behind and passing into the wild library that lived behind them. Here the shelves were arranged in clusters, squares and rings and pentagons, and were mostly empty. Strange noises and even smells leaked out of the gaps between them—the clatter of metal, the cheer of a crowd, the scent of roasting meat.

Inside each cluster was a book, or a set of books that shared similar characteristics. Portal-books and prison-books were not like ordinary volumes or the tomes in which Alice founds fragments of magic for Geryon to extract. They were nothing *but* magic, and—under a

Reader's gaze—they were a pathway between one place and another, one *world* and another. Left alone, they *leaked*. Part of Ending's job as guardian of the library was to arrange these clusters of shelves that in some way kept the books contained and prevented their inhabitants from wandering about.

The inside of each cluster tended to reflect the environment on the other side of the portal. They were like little worlds unto themselves, usually much larger on the inside than they looked from the outside, although mere spatial impossibilities had ceased to really surprise Alice. She found the cluster she was looking for—it was marked on the outside with a complicated rune, but she could smell the rich, wet scent of it yards away in any case—and squeezed herself into a gap between the shelves. Though it looked like it was only a few inches wide, she fit easily.

Inside, the backs of the shelves resembled a ring of stone monoliths surrounding a clearing a couple of hundred yards across. About half of it was occupied by a pond, and an enormous waterfall poured into it, filling the air with its splash and roar. Around the edges of the pond, jungle trees grew dense and thick, wound round with hanging vines and lianas. Huge, thick green leaves hung everywhere, dripping with moisture, and interwoven with sprays of tiny, wildly colored flowers, like miniature fireworks. It was hot enough that Alice started to sweat almost immediately.

Her logical mind wondered where the waterfall came from—the source was lost in the mists—or where the water went when it drained off. Inside the library, though, such questions simply didn't apply. Ending took care of it, as she took care of everything.

In the center of the little jungle was a circle of flagstones, cracked and overgrown with grass and flowers. In the middle of the circle there was, of course, a book, a thick, ancient-looking thing bound in green leather. Alice had left it carefully alone during her visits here; reading even the first page would take her *through*. If it was a portal-book, that wouldn't be so bad, she'd be able to return by the same route; but if it was a prison-book, there was no way out except by defeating the prisoner. One lesson that both Geryon and Ending had drummed into her was never to open a book if you didn't know what was on the other side.

The magic that leaked through, even while the book was closed, had gradually created this sprawl of jungle, and it was that energy Alice hoped to capture. She'd gathered a handful of acorns out in the woods and brought them here, priming them with a careful tweak of the tree-sprite's power. They would drink in the magic until they were full to bursting, and then Alice would able to call on them when she needed to.

That was the theory, at least. Getting the little tweak right proved harder than she'd thought. This was the third batch—the dozen acorns in her first two tries had variously sprouted into miniature trees, decomposed into necrotic slime, or simply exploded like tiny grenades when she'd picked them up, lodging bits of nutshell in her skin. Each attempt had to be left to soak for a week, so experimenting was a slow process.

In this batch, laid out in a neat ring around the book, she could see two of the little short-lived oak trees, and the one nearer her seemed to have transformed into a small patch of mushrooms. The other three looked intact, though, and she wondered if she'd finally gotten it right. Ending, while tremendously knowledgeable, could only *describe* what she had to do, not actually demonstrate it—using the powers of bound creatures was magic for Readers alone.

Ending's voice, a deep velvet purr, reached Alice's ear as though summoned by her thoughts. "Hello, Alice."

Alice kept herself from jumping only by strenuous

effort. As usual, the only sign of Ending was a pair of huge yellow eyes at a level with Alice's own, staring out of the deep shadow of the undergrowth. Beneath them, Ending's long fangs were just a hint of an ivory gleam.

"Hello," Alice said, keeping her voice calm.

In spite of their familiarity, there was always something unnerving about Ending. For one thing, while Alice had never seen her in the light, the glimpses she'd caught of paws or tail hinted at a black cat the size of a tiger. But it was more than that—Alice had faced plenty of monsters, but even the ugliest didn't match the sense of casual power Ending exuded. The library was her domain—in here she could see everything and be everywhere. *Or at least she would like me to think so.*

"It looks like it may have worked this time," she went on, when the cat didn't say anything. "Unless they explode again."

"It feels right this time," Ending said.

"Still, better safe than sorry," Alice muttered.

She pulled the Swarm thread around herself, hardening her skin, and went over to the acorns. When she nudged one with her foot, it didn't burst, so she bent down and picked it up. Tugging just a bit on the tree-sprite's thread let her feel the power coiled inside it, enough raw energy to create a full-grown tree squished into a nut that fit in her pocket. Alice closed her hand around it and grinned. The tree-sprite was one of her most useful creatures, but only if there were trees about to work with. Now she could bring her trees with her.

"Congratulations," Ending said as Alice picked up the other two acorns. "I knew you would get it eventually."

"Thank you for your help," Alice said politely.

"Now you've got a trick Geryon doesn't know about," Ending said. "I'm sure that will come in handy."

The thought of Geryon, and their conversation this morning, instantly obliterated Alice's good mood. It must have showed on her face, because Ending made a noise like "Hmm?" Her yellow eyes closed and vanished, appearing again in another patch of shadow close to Alice's side.

"What is it, child?" the cat purred. "Has something happened?"

"No," Alice said. "That's just it. Nothing's happened at all." She hesitated, not sure if she should talk about it. But Ending had helped her capture Vespidian, and already knew most of the story. "I asked Geryon if he'd found out anything about what happened to my father."

"And he said nothing," Ending said.

"He said he's looking into it. Asking the other old Readers."

Ending's brief snort was eloquent. Alice's cheeks heated.

"You think he isn't doing anything?" she said.

"Whether he is or not is of little consequence. The Readers are as miserly with their information as they are with their magic, and they give up neither simply for the asking. Besides, does Geryon truly want to find out? Suppose he discovered who was involved—what then? Does he go to war with another Reader on your behalf?"

Alice wasn't sure *what* would happen then. If her father was alive, then she would go to war to get him back, if that was what it took. Just finding out the truth had seemed so difficult, she hadn't thought much on what to do afterward.

"I think you're right," she said. "He seems more interested in figuring out how Vespidian found me, and you and I already know the answer to that."

"And speak of the devil," Ending said, then chuckled. "Our large friend has come to find you."

"Mr. Black?" Alice asked, surprised.

"Yes." Teeth gleamed as the cat yawned. "He's looking for you."

"I'd better go," Alice said.

"Much as I'm tempted to keep the lummox wandering around for hours, you're right." Ending let out a low rumble. "Interesting. Geryon wants the library locked down and the defenses checked. Something serious must have happened."

Alice guessed that Ending had a mental link to communicate with Geryon, as she did with her own creatures. "Is something attacking us?"

"Not yet. But whatever he wants you for . . ." Ending paused. "Be careful, child."

"I'm always careful."

"Be *very* careful. Now go and find Mr. Black before he gets frustrated and starts breaking things."

Alice nodded. She patted her pocket to reassure herself that the three acorns were still there, and hiked to the edge of the clearing, pushing through the jungle to one of the narrow gaps between the monolith/shelves. On the outside, she started walking back the way she'd come. Only a couple of turns later, she was back among the orderly shelves of the mundane library, and the next aisle she took led her directly to Mr. Wurms' table.

"I told you," came Mr. Wurms' voice, as dry and dusty as the old scholar himself. "I haven't seen her."

"Daft girl," Mr. Black rumbled. "Always wandering where she's not wanted—"

Alice stepped out from behind the shelves and cleared her throat, and they both turned to face her. Mr. Wurms worked at the intersection of two wide aisles, where he had a long trestle table piled high with books. Some of the stacks looked precarious, and most of them were covered with a thick layer of dust, as if they hadn't been touched in a long time. Mr. Wurms himself was normally draped in dust too, bent over his table for days at a time, only his quill pen *scritch-scritch-scritch*ing through stacks of yellow paper.

Mr. Black loomed next to the frail-looking scribe. He was tall and massively broad in the shoulders, and a wild mane of black hair, beard, and mustache gave his face a bestial appearance, with only his eyes visible. Those eyes narrowed when he saw Alice, and he shifted uncomfortably.

Ever since Alice had confronted him, Mr. Black had tried to avoid her entirely. Since he mostly worked in the furnace room, that was not difficult. When she did run into him, she'd found his dark looks tempered with a touch of disbelief, as though he were surprised she'd kept her word about not betraying his part in the scheme to Geryon. If they had to talk, he gave her a wary respect, although she was under no illusion that he was truly friendly.

"Miss Alice," he said, in his deep rumble of a voice. "So you're here after all."

"*I* haven't seen you," Mr. Wurms said querulously. "I've things that need fetching."

"I'm sorry," Alice said. "I took a bit of a wrong turn."

Mr. Wurms sniffed, but it was hard to argue with that excuse. Unless Ending was paying you special attention, finding things even in the mundane side of the library wasn't easy.

"You'll have to do your own fetching, or wait a bit longer," Mr. Black said. "The girl's to come to the house right away. Master's orders."

Mr. Wurms gave the long-suffering sigh of the eternally put-upon, but raised no argument. Mr. Black beckoned, and Alice fell in beside him, having to take two hurried steps to match each of his long strides.

"Do you know what's going on?" she ventured, once they'd left Mr. Wurms behind.

"Something dangerous," Mr. Black said. "Master's got

all the wards turned up as high as they'll go; that takes a lot of power."

"He didn't tell you why?"

"Nope." She thought he was smiling, but it was hard to tell under his shaggy beard. "Lucky you, you get to find out."

CHAPTER FOUR

UNEXPECTED NEWS

GERYON SAT IN HIS study, in one of four high-backed armchairs that faced one another in front of the fireplace. The muddy stain from where Alice had emerged from the swamp was gone.

"Sorry to take so long, sir," Alice said. "I was deep in the library, and it took Mr. Black some time to find me." The huge servant had left her at the entrance to Geryon's suite, muttering to himself as he retreated to his basement sanctuary.

"Fortunately, we have a little time." Geryon gestured for her to sit. She did, perching on the edge of one of the overstuffed seats, her feet not quite reaching the ground. "I've had some interesting news."

"News?" Her chest tightened for a moment.

Geryon nodded. By this of course he meant news from *his* world, something that had happened among the Readers. Mere human happenings—that President Hoover had been assassinated, say, or that an earthquake had sunk Rhode Island into the sea—would not concern him. *Has he heard something about Father?* But his expression was all wrong for that, and she forced herself to be calm.

"Indeed. The gravest kind." Geryon paused. "One of my colleagues is dead."

Alice had picked up enough to have an idea of how serious this was. Geryon's "colleagues" were the small group that Alice thought of as the old Readers at the top of the hierarchy of the magical world. They were all ancient—avoiding the perils of old age was apparently small potatoes for a sufficiently skilled Reader—and engaged in a complicated game of negotiation, alliance, and betrayal that stretched back through the centuries like a tangled spiderweb.

Alice had devoted some thought to this, in the small hours of the night. She was a Reader too, which presumably meant she could live forever, the same as Geryon. It was a difficult concept to get her mind around. She had a hard enough time imagining herself at twenty, let alone two hundred or two thousand.

In any case, the death of an old Reader was an event that would shake the delicate arrangement of relationships to its core. It was a given that he'd been killed, of course. There was no other way for an old Reader *to* die.

"I . . . see." In other circumstances, Alice might have asked if the dead man had been a friend of Geryon's, but the old Readers did not have friends, only tools and allies. Instead, because it was the kind of thing he liked to hear, she said, "Does this affect us?"

"Very much so, I'm afraid. The colleague I refer to is named Esau-of-the-Waters, and he has—*had*," he corrected himself, "close ties to me and several other Readers of my acquaintance. And the manner of his death . . ."

Esau-of-the-Waters? Alice sat up a little straighter, fighting hard to keep her expression neutral. *Could that be a coincidence?* Esau, as Vespidian's master, had been her only remaining hope of finding out what happened. The thought that she might *never* know for certain if her father was truly dead filled her with panic. She clenched her fists until her knuckles went white.

She couldn't tell if Geryon noticed her agitation. He seemed distracted, scratching his cheek with one finger and then smoothing out the whiskers again. He paused for a long time, but Alice knew better than to prompt him.

"The manner of his death," the old Reader said again, "is disturbing. As best we can tell, he was murdered by his apprentice." His eyes found hers, and a faint smile played at the corner of his mouth. "You seem shocked."

Alice took a deep breath and calmed herself with an effort. "It's just hard to imagine, sir."

"Is it? It's not without precedent. We try to choose our students carefully, but so few are born with the talent, and sometimes a Reader will take a chance on a . . . questionable individual. And, of course, even the most careful man tends to lower his guard around his own apprentices. But I must admit I was surprised to hear it in this case. Esau was a very careful man indeed."

"What happened to the apprentice?"

"Ah, Alice. You have, as usual, gone straight to the heart of the matter. We believe the boy—his name is Jacob—is still hiding in Esau's fortress. Or possibly he is trapped there, it's not clear. Either way, he must be dealt with." He broke off. "It can't be pleasant for you to hear this, I know, but as one of us, you'll have to face this kind of unpleasantness eventually. An apprentice who commits some offense is normally chastised by his own master, as he sees fit. But in a case like this one, it falls to the rest of us to administer . . . justice."

"I see, sir," Alice said, though she didn't, quite.

"We must act together, to demonstrate solidarity of purpose. In such circumstances each Reader sends an apprentice to deal with the guilty party."

"You're sending me to . . . deal with him?"

Geryon's lips tightened. "You will go to Esau's fortress with a small group of apprentices from the other Readers who share an interest in the situation. You will find Jacob, apprehend him, and bring him back for judgment. If that can be accomplished without violence, so much the better. If not, you will do what you must."

Alice looked back at him, chewing her lip. *It won't be in a prison-book. We won't have to kill him.*

What's the difference? a dark part of her mind whispered. *You know what the old Readers will do to him if you bring him back.*

But he did murder someone. It wasn't like you could call the police to a Reader's fortress. *Someone has to do something.*

Geryon caught her expression, but misread the source of her hesitation.

"Breaking into the fortress should not be too difficult," he said. "There will be others in the group with more . . . experience, and whatever pacts and wards Esau created to defend his domain will not have survived his death. That is part of the problem, in fact. Like all of us, Esau accumulated a great many powerful books during his life, and without his defenses in place, they will gradually begin to run rampant in the labyrinth. The wayward apprentice must be removed so that we can send our servants to contain the mess."

"I understand, sir." She wanted to ask more questions, but Geryon's expression told her he would not be receptive. "When will I be going?"

"This afternoon. Gather whatever you need." He made a dismissive motion with one hand. "I will call you when the time comes."

"What I don't understand," Alice said to Ashes as they climbed the stairs toward her room, "is why he doesn't go himself."

"The same reason he hardly ever leaves the house. He's

afraid of the other Readers. None of them trust the others farther than they can spit. Getting two of them in one place is the next best thing to starting a fight already. If you tried to gather five or six, there'd be nothing left but a smoking crater. That's why they *have* apprentices."

Ashes rubbed his head against her ankle as she stopped in front of her door. "Look, no offense, but you're pretty young as apprentices go. You've got a lot of talent, but there'll be stronger kids than you in the group. You just need to go along for the ride."

Alice paused, with her hand on the latch. "Then why's he sending me at all?"

"To keep an eye on the others, of course." Ashes sniffed. "And maybe to make sure you're properly scared, in case you ever get ideas about trying what Jacob did. But it's not *justice* that they're mostly concerned with, it's division of the loot. All you apprentices are mostly there to watch one another and make sure nobody tries to sneak anything out."

It took a moment for Alice to process this. Her head was still spinning, and she shook it to try and clear some of the cobwebs.

"Wait here. I've got to change."

Ashes, obedient for once, curled up against the opposite wall. Alice shut the door behind her and leaned against it, trying to make sense of things.

Her little room hadn't changed much since she'd first arrived. The two stuffed rabbits, all she had left of the old house where she'd live with her father, still kept their silent vigil on the windowsill. She went over and pulled one of them into her lap.

She could refuse to go, she supposed, but Geryon would punish her—she wasn't quite sure *how*; she'd never truly made him angry, but her imagination could supply particulars all too readily—and the wayward apprentice, Jacob, would be hunted down anyway.

And, though it made her uncomfortable to be part of a . . . a *posse*, like in some cinema Western, she wasn't entirely sure she didn't want to go. *There may be something in Esau's fortress that can tell me the truth about my father. Some record, or one of his creatures. This could be my only chance.*

Once the Readers had divvied up his treasures, like the creditors who'd swooped in on her father's house after his ship went down, she'd never be able to find what she was looking for.

But what if we do find Jacob, and somehow it's up to me

to fight him? If he attacked her, she supposed she would fight back. But she wasn't certain she could attack a person if he just refused to come with her. *Could I stand by and watch while someone else does it? Isn't that just as bad?*

She couldn't shake the feeling that there was more to it than Geryon was saying. It was all very well to say Jacob had murdered his master, but *how?* In spite of what Geryon had said, it was hard to picture someone like Esau—who'd lived for God-knows-how-long by virtue of caution and paranoia—lowering his guard enough for a mere apprentice to get the advantage of him. *And why would Jacob do it?* He had to know what the other old Readers would do to him.

I can talk to Jacob, she decided. *Perhaps he's mad. Or perhaps he had a good reason, and he can explain things to Geryon and the others. And if I can get him alone, maybe he can answer my questions too.*

Chapter Five
THE CAVE OF DOORS

ALICE DRESSED IN HER usual outfit for expeditions: sturdy, boyish trousers, a belt hung with handy pouches, and a coat suitable for rugged outdoor work. She stuffed the pouches with a few things she'd found useful in emergencies: matches, bandages, extra socks, and the three special acorns from the library. Lastly, she added a knife, in a leather sheath on her hip. She thought of this as a tool, rather than a weapon. If she ever *were* inclined to kill someone, Alice reflected, these days she hardly needed a knife to do it.

Ashes swung his tail approvingly as she emerged, circling around her feet and brushing against her ankles.

"You look like a proper little wildcat now," he said.

"Remember the night we met? Sneaking into the library in your nightshirt and one slipper?"

Alice didn't dignify that with a response. She headed for the stairs, and Ashes padded along behind her. Truthfully, though, she did feel—competent, perhaps? Even a little dangerous. The threads hummed at the back of her mind, tense with latent power. *Look out, world.* She grinned, feeling suddenly ridiculous, and shook her head.

Geryon greeted her at the door to his suite. He frowned at Ashes.

"I'll be raising the wards," he said to the cat. "So you'll have to stay outside."

Alice knelt down and scratched Ashes behind the ears—something he enjoyed, even if he wouldn't admit it.

"Don't do anything silly," he said, soft enough that Geryon couldn't hear. "I won't be there to rescue you this time when it all goes wrong."

Alice smiled. "I'll do my best."

"Ashes," Geryon snapped.

He heaved a feline sigh and coiled away, all wounded dignity, tail flicking back and forth behind him. Geryon stepped out of the way and let Alice through, then closed and locked the door behind them.

"Every Reader keeps a single open portal into his fortress," Geryon said as they walked down the corridor. "A front door, if you like. Most of us maintain many other portals as well, of course, but this one is for official business. The place it leads to is heavily warded and alarmed, so it's impossible for one of us to use it to sneak up on the others. That helps prevent . . . misunderstandings."

He stopped at the door that led to his vault and placed his hand against it. Something inside the room clicked, and the door swung open.

"Of course," he added, "I keep the portal carefully locked away in any event. Better safe than sorry."

Alice peered around the corner. The dog-spider-thing she remembered from when Isaac had broken in was gone, and if another guardian had replaced it, it wasn't visible. The shelves full of chests were still there, though, and Geryon went to a corner and picked up one of the smallest lockboxes. It was a solid metal cube, with no visible hinges and only a slight bulge to suggest a lock. Geryon tapped the protrusion with his finger, and the shiny surface rippled like still water broken by a flung pebble. A circle in the top of the box dissolved into thin air, revealing an interior lined with red velvet. A thin book, barely more than a pamphlet, lay inside.

Geryon lifted it out and handed it to Alice, pressing his hands around hers for a moment. His skin was rough, and he smelled of ink and the weird, too-sweet concoction he used for gluing and binding new books.

"I want you to be careful," he said. "Don't take any unnecessary risks."

"I thought you said it wouldn't be dangerous."

"Assaulting a Reader's fortress by the front door would be *impossible*," he corrected. "With the defenses gone, I said it would not be difficult. But there may still be dangers. Creatures from the books will have found their way into the world, and some of them will be hostile."

"Ah."

"And you must watch your fellow apprentices. If any of them attempt to steal books or treasures from the fortress, report them to me, and their master and I will . . . have words." The old Reader cleared his throat. "I don't anticipate outright treachery. But every Reader trains his students as he sees fit, and not all of them are as liberal in their approach as I am. Remain alert."

"Yes, sir." A thought occurred to Alice. "Will they speak English, sir? If they're from all over . . ."

"Not 'all over,' in this case. Only those who had close dealings with Esau will send representatives," Geryon said, as though he'd genuinely forgotten the problem. He smiled gently. "It matters very little. Do you think Ashes learned English as a kitten?"

"I . . . I hadn't considered it, sir."

"It's only humans who suffer from the curse of Babel. The words of Readers, and magical creatures, carry pure *meaning*. Suffice to say that if you wish to be understood, you will be, and vice versa."

"I see, sir. That's good to know."

"Be polite and respectful," Geryon said. "But do not grow too friendly with the others. Remember that, however you may feel toward one another personally, they must obey their masters, and the will of those masters may set them against you someday. It does not serve to become too attached to those who may eventually be your enemies."

Isaac had said something similar to her, the last time they'd seen each other. *I wonder if he'll be there?* She had no idea if his master, Anaxomander, had had "close dealings" with Esau, but it would be nice to see a familiar face. *Even if I still owe him a punch on the nose.*

"I understand, sir."

"Very well. Good luck. I will be waiting for your return."

Alice nodded, and flipped open the book. As usual,

there was a moment where the letters were a mass of flickering, incomprehensible light, and then they twisted and resolved under her gaze.

She read, *The air smelled musty and damp, like cold, wet stone . . .*

The air smelled musty and damp, like cold, wet stone. A faint breeze was chilly against her cheek, and she could hear the *plink, plink* of dripping water in the distance. It reminded her of the world of the Swarm, but only for a moment. The rough floor under her boots felt like natural stone, not bricks, and there was none of the faint sewer smell of that place, just the clean scent of ancient rock.

Even after Alice counted to fifty, her eyes still hadn't adjusted to the utter darkness. She reached out with her mind for the devilfish thread and tugged, summoning the creature's ghostly glow. It cast weird, green-tinted shadows.

She was, as she'd guessed, in a cave. It was roughly circular, big enough to hold a couple of tennis courts, with the ceiling perhaps twenty feet overhead. There was no way in or out that she could see. A couple of the walls had long cracks, and she could feel a steady breath of fresh air through them.

Lining the wall of the cave was a row of boulders, too

evenly spaced to be natural. One of them was right behind her, and she could see a duplicate of the little book she'd come in through. Engraved on the rock was a single rune, which, while unfamiliar, nevertheless carried the meaning *Geryon* as clearly to Alice as if it were spelled out in familiar Roman characters.

Those must be the other "front doors," she thought, looking around at the other boulders. There were more of them than she'd expected, at least fifty. Curious, Alice went to the one beside Geryon's. She could see where a rune had once been, but someone had chiseled it through with deep cuts. No book lay above it.

She raised her glowing hand above her head and looked around the room for any sign of the other apprentices she was supposed to meet. Nothing moved except for shadows. Maybe I'm early.

She started walking the circle, looking at each rune in turn and parsing its meaning. *Helian. Coldheart. Jezail. Vin Einarson. Master of the Closed Circle.* Each of them had their own book, in a variety of shapes and sizes. Alice didn't venture too close, for fear of tripping magical alarms. There were more empty spaces too, names scratched out and pedestals empty.

Before she'd gone a quarter of the way around the circle, a light appeared ahead of her, cheerful and yellow against the green glow from the devilfish. Alice squinted and made out a figure carrying a lantern. She waved her glowing hand, and the light bobbed in response. Encouraged, she went closer.

"Hello," Alice said. "Are you here for the expedition?"

"I am!" It was a girl's voice, with an odd, lilting accent. "And you must be one of our company as well!"

The other girl raised her lantern higher, throwing back the shadows. She was Alice's age or a little older, with dark skin and black, frizzy hair tied back. Her clothes were strange: a sack-like robe of pure white fabric tied at her hips and shoulders to leave her limbs free, and sandals secured by a complicated web of straps. She greeted Alice with a broad smile.

"I am glad to meet you, sister," the girl said, giving a formal-looking half bow. "May auspicious signs shine on our endeavor."

This caught Alice a bit off guard. She nodded as politely as she could.

"It's nice to meet you too," she said eventually. "I'm Alice."

"Alice!" the girl said delightedly. "From *Adalheidis*, signifying nobility of being or birth. Most promising. I am Dexithea, named after the Telchine, though of course there is no true relation." Alice's confusion must have been visible, because the girl added, "On previous expeditions my companions have found it convenient to address me as Dex. Please do so if you wish!"

"Dex," Alice said. "Got it." She paused. "You've done this kind of thing before?"

"Indeed. My master, the Most Favored, has sent me to venture out with my brothers and sisters whenever the stars favor it. Though never, I must admit, to punish one of our own." Her smile faded slightly, then brightened again. "This is your first outing of this sort?"

"More or less," Alice said. She didn't think her trek through the library with Isaac really counted.

"Then I am glad I was the first to greet you!" Dex shook her head. "Some of our brothers and sisters worry more than is good for them. First meetings can sometimes be rather tense affairs."

"It's called a healthy paranoia," a deep voice growled just behind Alice. "And frankly, you could stand to develop a little more of it."

CHAPTER SIX
THE GANG'S ALL HERE

Instinctively, Alice yanked at the Swarm thread, pulling it inside her to make her skin tough and rubbery. She dove forward, rolled across the rocky floor, and came up in a crouch a few yards away.

Where she'd been standing, there was ... a shadow. A patch of shadow, solid and three-dimensional, boiling in the direct glow of the devilfish. Scraps of darkness flapped like ribbons of black silk in a gale, coming loose and dissolving into nothing, replenished by a constant upwelling of shadow from below. From this strange thing came the sound of—

Laughter?

"I'm sorry," said the voice, apparently from nowhere.

"I know I shouldn't do that. It's just so cute watching new kids jump."

The shadow dissolved, breaking apart into a storm of flying scraps that fizzled into black sparks, like a photo-negative of a spitting fire. In its place was a tall, pale young man in a black silk cloak, smiling broadly but, Alice thought, with more than a bit of malice in his eyes. He had a long face and light brown hair, which he wore slicked back in a careful part. She guessed he was sixteen or seventeen.

Alice straightened up, slowly, and let the Swarm thread slip away. She glared at him, wishing she didn't have to look quite so far up to do so. There was something about his grin that she wanted to hit with something heavy. She took a business-like tone.

"You really shouldn't," she said. "I could easily have hurt you."

"Next time I'll be sure to announce myself," he said, still grinning, and took the edge of his cloak in hand to make a pretentious bow. "Garret Arcane, at your service. You have my apologies, Miss . . . "

"Creighton," Alice said. "Alice Creighton."

"And Dex," Garret said. "You're looking well, considering."

"Of course," Dex said. "The Most Favored was able to

reattach the arm you so thoughtfully retrieved for me." She held up her arm to the lantern light, showing a thick band of shiny scar tissue just above the elbow. "See? Good as new."

"Glad to hear it." Garret caught Alice's expression and winked. "Sometimes these little trips can get a bit rough. But I'll take care of you, never fear. Any sign of the others?"

"I haven't seen anyone," Alice said.

"Ah, but you didn't see me, did you?" Garret grinned. "Healthy paranoia, like I said. What if I'd been something horrible?"

Before Alice could think of a response, sudden light bloomed on the other side of the cavern, followed by a girl's voice, shouting. She couldn't make out the words, but Garret rolled his eyes theatrically.

"That'll be Ellen, being her usual charming self," he said. "Come on. We'd better sort it out or they'll kill each other before we even get started."

Garret led the way across the cavern. Alice, walking beside Dex, couldn't help staring at the scar on her arm. When Dex caught her looking, Alice cleared her throat uncomfortably.

"I was just wondering what happened," she said.

Dex smiled. "I encountered some difficulty during a joint expedition into one of the Lower Third Septieth worlds."

"She fell into a swamp," Garret said from up ahead, "and a giant crocodile-thing bit it *off*."

"Bit it off?" Alice said.

"Fortunately Brother Garret was kind enough to lend me his assistance," Dex said. "All's well that ends well."

"But didn't that hurt?"

Dex shrugged. "Pain is an illusion. The body is only a clay vessel holding the immortal essence of the soul, so it is a mistake to attach any import to the difficulties it may encounter. In fact, the whole episode reinforced my fundamental understanding of—" She caught Alice's expression. "Yes. It hurt quite a lot."

Garret pulled up short, shading his eyes with one hand. The light had grown steadily brighter as they approached, until it was almost too intense to look at.

"Ellen!" he shouted. "Is that you?"

A girl's voice came back. "Garret? I ought to have guessed you'd be here."

"You know me, I never miss a party," Garret said. "Would you mind turning your halo down a few notches before you blind everybody?"

The brilliant light dimmed to a more comfortable level, and Alice could see the girl who stood underneath it. She was tall and skinny, with short blond hair and pale skin. Alice guessed she was the same age as Garret. Her outfit looked a bit like Alice's, durable and practical, though it had seen considerably more use.

"Is that Dex with you?" Ellen said.

"Yup," Garret said. "And this is—"

"Alice," Alice interrupted.

"She's new," Garret added.

"There's another girl around here somewhere," Ellen said. "But I barely got a look at her before she ran off."

"I'm not surprised, with you shining that searchlight around," Garret said. "Anybody would be frightened."

Ellen scowled. The light—which emanated from thin air a foot above her head—rippled and brightened, as if in response to her anger. "That's hardly my fault. She startled me."

"I'll find her." Garret raised a hand, and wisps of shadow started to gather around him.

Ellen rolled her eyes. "Oh yes, sneak up behind her. I'm sure that will help."

The shadows paused. "You're not still sore that I caught you last time?"

"Of course not." Ellen sniffed. "And you did *not* catch me."

"Oh, come on. You must have jumped five feet!"

"It's a perfectly rational reaction when you're waiting in some nasty bog and you hear something moving behind you."

"And you screamed."

"I did *not*—"

"Oh, for goodness' sake," Alice said. "Which way did she go?"

The two older apprentices paused their argument to look at her. Ellen pointed, and Alice nodded curtly and brushed past them. Dex caught her eye and flashed a grin where the other two couldn't see.

Their bickering resumed behind her as Alice walked out into the darkness. She pulled gently on the devilfish thread, summoning the soft green glow, and walked slowly around the ring of boulders. Aside from the rocks, the cave wall was smooth, and there didn't seem to be anywhere to hide.

"Hello?" Alice said. "I'm sorry if they scared you. We're not going to hurt you, I promise." She paused to look behind one of the rocks, and found nothing. "Hello? Are you there?"

A flash of motion caught her eye. Alice looked around in time to see a small girl take a long step away from the cave wall and gasp for air, as though she'd just broken the surface after a long swim underwater. She hadn't been there a moment before, Alice was certain.

She was a tiny, frail-looking thing, a few inches shorter than Alice and painfully thin. Everything she wore was made of leather, a vest and short pants that didn't reach her knees, so haphazardly stitched that Alice wondered if she'd made the clothes herself. Her mouse-brown hair was pinned up on the right, but the other side she let fall in a long, straight curtain that touched her shoulder and obscured that half of her face.

Alice forced herself to remain still. The whole of the girl's tiny body vibrated with tension, ready to turn and flee.

"Hello," Alice said, in the most reassuring voice she could manage. "It's all right. I'm not going to hurt you."

"I saw the light," the girl said, in a voice so low it was almost a whisper. "And I thought . . ." She blinked, and shook her head. Her stance relaxed a fraction, and Alice nodded encouragingly.

"I'm Alice," she said. "You're new at this like me, aren't you?"

"Yes," the girl said, after a moment's careful consideration.

"What's your name?" Alice prompted.

"Soranna."

"That's a nice name."

There was another silence. Alice found herself somewhat at sea with this strange girl who spoke in monosyllables. In the days before Alice had come to Geryon's—which now felt like memories from another lifetime—she'd never been comfortable around children, preferring the company of adults. She based her manner on the slow gentle tone taken by grown-ups who didn't know her, which she'd always privately thought sounded like someone talking to a lapdog.

"Why don't you come back and meet the others?" Alice said. "They're all very nice, and they won't hurt you either." She paused, compelled to be honest. "At least, I hope that they're nice, I've only just met them. But I'm pretty sure they won't hurt you."

The girl narrowed her eyes, but nodded. Alice led her back toward Ellen's light, which was shifting and brightening as she continued her argument with Garret. The raised voices made Soranna hesitate, and Alice encouraged her with a smile.

"Sister Alice!" Dex said. "I see that you have retrieved our wayward lamb."

Soranna gave Dex an alarmed look, but held her ground.

"Her name's Soranna," Alice said.

Ellen looked the little girl over, clearly unimpressed. She sniffed and turned away.

"Little Sora," Garret said, with an affected joviality. "Good to meet you."

"Soranna," said Soranna sharply. "*Not* Sora."

Garret blinked. "All right. Soranna it is."

"Is this everyone?" Ellen said. "I'd like to get on with it."

"My master told me to expect five others," Garret said. "Maybe someone's running late."

"Well, I certainly don't plan on waiting around here all day," Ellen said. "I say we give it another five minutes."

"There is strength in numbers," Dex said. "Better not to venture forth unprepared."

"We'll be fine," Ellen said. "I'm sure the three of us can handle whatever is in there." Then, as an afterthought, she added, "And Alice and Sora will help too, of course."

"Soranna," Soranna said. "Not Sora."

"Ellen's right," Garret said. "I'm not worried. But if we leave without someone, the masters might not like it."

"Then his master should have gotten him here on time," Ellen said. "I think—"

"I'm here," said a familiar voice from the darkness. A boy stepped forward, swathed in an ancient, battered trench coat.

"Isaac!" Alice took a half step forward, then stopped when he refused to meet her eyes. He brushed right past her and took up a slouching position beside Garret.

"Isaac," Garret said. "Good to see you again. You're looking—"

"I'm here," Isaac repeated, keeping his eyes on the ground. "Let's go."

Garret glanced at Ellen, who shrugged dismissively.

"That appears to complete our company!" Dex said brightly. "May the most favorable of portents attend our journey."

Ellen made a face, but said nothing. Garret beckoned everyone over to the nearest boulder, which Alice now saw was inscribed with the name *Esau-of-the-Waters*.

"All right," Garret said. "For those of you who haven't done this before, just stay close and keep your heads down. We're not expecting any active opposition, but some nasty things may have already gotten loose from

Esau's archives. Follow me and watch the sides—"

"Who exactly put you in charge?" Ellen snapped.

"Follow *Ellen and me*"—Garret amended. Ellen sniffed and crossed her arms—"who will be out in front in case something happens. Dex, you bring up the rear."

Alice cleared her throat. "What about when we find Jacob?"

Garret shrugged, and cracked his knuckles ostentatiously. "That depends on whether he feels like coming along quietly."

Ellen rolled her eyes. "Leave him to us. We'll handle it."

Alice thought she saw Isaac flinch. She tried to catch his eye, but he looked away.

"Okay!" Garret said. "Everybody join hands. We'll all go through together."

He held out his hand, and Isaac took it, reluctantly. Alice ended up between Ellen and Soranna, the former barely touching her fingers, the latter squeezing as hard as if she were afraid of falling. Soranna's fingers were rough and calloused.

Garret flipped open the book that sat on the boulder, a fat, narrow tome with an ancient leather binding. Alice was too far away to read it, but she could feel the meaning flow through her, down the line of linked hands. The words swam into their vision.

Alice found herself outside, under a night sky ablaze with starlight . . .

CHAPTER SEVEN
ESAU'S FORTRESS

ALICE FOUND HERSELF OUTSIDE, under a night sky ablaze with starlight. There were more stars than she'd ever seen, more even than were in the sky at the Library, far from the glow of civilization. In every direction except above, there was only darkness, black and absolute. The shadows of huge mountain peaks were visible where they blotted out chunks of the sky, a set of jagged, sharp-edged shapes like a row of shark's teeth. They surrounded her on all sides, as though she stood in the center of a giant pair of earthen jaws preparing to take a bite out of the heavens.

She released Ellen's hand and tried to disentangle herself from Soranna, but the girl seemed reluctant. Alice gave her a reassuring squeeze.

"Where are we?" she said.

Ellen's halo brightened, enough to show that they stood on a small stone platform surrounded by an iron railing. A single gate led onto a narrow stone walkway that stretched off into the darkness. When Alice squinted, she could see that there were lights in that direction, faint and flickering, like the glow of a distant campfire.

"Somewhere in the Alps," Ellen said. "My master said Esau carved out a valley between the mountains and built his fortress in it, then wrapped it around with wards so the mortals would never find it." She glanced up at the sky. "And it's always night here, no matter what happens outside."

"I wonder how long that will keep working," Garret said. "Now that he's dead, I mean. It depends on the power draw—"

Ellen pointed to the distant lights. "That must be the fortress. If this is his front door, it makes sense that he'd keep it at a safe distance."

Alice walked to the edge of the platform and put her hands on the railing. She was glad she'd worn something warm; the air was thin and chill, and the metal cold against her skin. She pulled on the devilfish thread and summoned the luminescent green glow.

An involuntary gasp escaped her, and her hands tightened on the iron. Beyond the rail was a sheer cliff that extended down for hundreds of feet. She couldn't see the bottom, and a dizzy sense of vertigo roiled her stomach and pricked at the soles of her feet. Slowly, Alice released the railing and took a careful step backward.

Garret had apparently made a similar discovery. "Nobody is to fall off," he said. "Unless you can fly. Come on, let's get moving."

He strode out onto the walkway, and Ellen fell in behind him. Her halo threw long, twisting shadows. Isaac hurried after them, leaving Alice in the rear with Dex and Soranna.

Dex edged to the side of the platform, looked down, and whistled.

"Don't fall off, Brother Garret says. Good advice indeed." She waved Alice forward. "Proceed, sisters. I will watch behind us."

Soranna looked miserable in the green devilfish light. Alice hesitated a moment, then held out her hand again, and the girl took it gratefully. Together they stepped out onto the walkway. It was comfortably wide, but there

were no railings along its sides, and the thought of that awful drop made Alice keep to the very center.

The stone path seemed to go on forever. The platform behind them soon vanished into darkness, leaving only the light of Dex's lantern, Alice's hand, and Ellen's halo bobbing ahead. The lights of the fortress, if that's what they were, weren't getting any closer. Soranna's hand was warm in Alice's.

Alice found herself wrestling with her feelings. On the one hand she was relieved, as it seemed unlikely she would have to make any decision about Jacob after all. It felt a bit cowardly to simply let Garret or Ellen handle everything, but it wasn't like they'd given her a choice in the matter. *Ashes was right. Geryon sent me here just to . . . show the flag, I suppose, and make sure none of the others get away with anything.*

On the other hand, just going along with the group *grated*, in a way she had a hard time explaining. She'd usually followed the rules, because they were *good* rules, set down by people who cared for her and knew better than she did. Part of the reason she and her father had gotten along so well was that he'd never demanded anything of her that she couldn't see the sense in.

She was certain Garret didn't care for her, and she

wasn't at all sure he knew better than she did. Alice bridled at his cocksure attitude, but she couldn't see what she could do other than follow. *And be* extra *careful.*

And then, on the other *other* hand—

If I'm going to find out what happened to my father, I can't just trail behind Garret and Ellen. My best chance is to find a way to talk to Jacob alone, and make him tell me if he knows anything. Or maybe Esau kept some kind of records?

She fixed her eyes on Ellen's light. Isaac was a shadowy figure, just behind it. *And what's wrong with him, anyway? I know we didn't exactly part on the best of terms*—she found herself unaccountably blushing—*but if anything, I should be angry with him! He's the one who stole the Dragon book.*

Maybe that was it, she reflected. *He thinks I'm furious with him, so he's staying away from me.* She certainly had every right to be. *But this isn't the time to be petty. We have to work together.* When she finally cornered him, she'd have to give him a fair chance to apologize.

Slowly, the constellation of lights ahead grew clearer, flickering on and off in a strange pattern. When they were close enough to see the softer glow of starlight reflecting on stone, it suddenly snapped into focus, and Alice gasped and pulled up short.

It was a castle. But not like any castle Alice had ever

seen, even in a book of fairy tales. It was composed of a series of tall, flat-roofed towers, connected by long walkways. They spread out, up and down, staircases, ramps, and slides connecting each tower to its neighbors and other, more distant towers in a dozen ways. The paths curled over and under one another, crisscrossing like the web of an insane spider cast in stone.

Torches hung in the many windows of the towers and along the walkways. But it was the starlight that revealed the most surprising thing: Each tower rested on a single rock spire, stretching up from the black depths of the crevasse below. The entire castle was perched on hundreds of these pillars, like a bed of needles.

In the center of the mass of towers, a single huge building rose, round and dome-roofed. More torches shone in a ring around it, like a crown of fire sitting on a bald stone head, and a hundred bridges stretched away from it to every level of the surrounding towers.

Alice became aware that the others had halted too. The six of them stood quietly for a moment, staring at the huge complex.

"Well," Garret said, "it's pretty obvious where we have to go." He pointed at the big central building. "That must be Esau's stronghold."

"That doesn't mean Jacob is in there," Ellen said. "If he has any brains at all, he'd hide in one of the outlying towers. Searching this place would take years!"

"I can help with that, Sister Ellen," Dex said. "Auguries and finding are my specialty."

Ellen sniffed. "Your last augury led us into a swamp."

"We did find what we sought."

"And nearly lost your arm."

Dex shrugged. "The signs tell me where the road leads, not what troubles we will face along the way."

"*In any case*," Garret broke in, "we should investigate the stronghold first. If he's not there, we'll widen our search."

"We'll have to get there first," Ellen said. "*Look* at this place. It's a maze."

A labyrinth.

This last was not spoken aloud. It was a low, resonant voice that echoed around Alice's skull and down to the pit of her stomach. It was a deeper, louder voice than any human's, but Alice recognized it, even after six months of silence. *That's not a day I'm ever likely to forget.*

The Dragon hadn't spoken a word since the day it had submitted to her, inside the prison-book. She'd never been able to pull its thread toward the world to summon or control it. It just sat there, deep in her mind, like a toad at the bottom of a pond.

Now she took hold of the thread. *Can you hear me?* she thought at it.

I can hear you, little sister.

A dozen questions came to mind. *Why haven't you spoken to me before now? Can Isaac hear you too?*

No. His mind is closed to me. And there was never a need before. But now you are in great danger.

Danger? She looked up at the castle. *Here?*

Yes. You are entering a labyrinth. If you continue, you are lost.

It might be hard to find our way through, but I'm sure we can remember the way out. Even as she thought it, though, she knew that wasn't what the Dragon meant.

This is no simple maze. It is a labyrinth. *The lair of one of the labyrinthine, the maze-demons.* The Dragon paused. *You know such a creature yourself.*

Ending. You mean Ending.

Yes. She serves Geryon, as all her kind must serve the Readers. They imprison the books of magic. Inside their labyrinth, they see all and control all.

Geryon said that all Esau's contracts would dissolve when he died, so we'd be safe.

They should have. But the labyrinthine remains at his post. I do not know why. But if you continue, you will be at his mercy.

Alice paused. Garret and Ellen had started forward again, toward the tower.

What should I do?

Turn back.

I don't think the others will want to.

If you continue, you will be trapped in the labyrinth. Most likely you will all die. The labyrinthine are not pleasant creatures, on the whole.

Ending seems nice enough, Alice thought defensively. *Sometimes, anyway.*

Something echoed from her mind, like a distant snort from vast nostrils. Then the Dragon's presence was gone. Alice kept her grip on the thread, but it was once again as hard as rock, and unresponsive to any of her entreaties.

Wait. I need to know . . .

But she could tell it was pointless, even without waiting for an answer.

CHAPTER EIGHT
INTO THE MAZE

THE WALKWAY LED TO an arched doorway in a gloomy-looking tower near the edge of the castle. A few torches cast weak pools of radiance out the windows, throwing long shadows. Inside, Alice could see a stone-floored chamber, with a long spiral stair winding around the inside of the wall. In the center was a messy heap of—

"Books?" Alice said aloud.

"Of course," Dex said. "Every master must have his library."

Geryon's books were at least *shelved*, even if they weren't sorted or organized. Here the volumes had simply been dumped in a pile like so much dross. Alice, looking at the folded pages and cracked spines, couldn't help but feel a bit sorry for them.

"No one is to touch anything," Garret said. "You know how it is. Our masters will send people to clean this place up, that's not our job. Besides, it could be dangerous."

Alice took a deep breath. She wasn't optimistic that Garret would heed her warning, but she couldn't just do *nothing*. Isaac might have listened, given his history with the Dragon, but Isaac was apparently not speaking to her.

"Garret?" she said as they paused just outside the doorway. "Can I have a word?"

Garret raised an eyebrow, but gestured her over to the side of the walkway, away from the others. Ellen followed without being invited.

"I've had . . ." Alice hesitated. "A warning. A sort of feeling, from one of my bound creatures. It says the labyrinth we're walking into is still active."

"An active labyrinth?" Garret looked up at the tower, and the maze of passages beyond. "Here?"

"That's not possible," Ellen said primly. "Esau's guardian would have left when he was killed. And an active labyrinth requires a guardian."

"I hate to say it, but Ellen's right," Garret said. "Our

masters wouldn't have sent us here if the labyrinth was still functioning. It'd be suicide."

Alice shrugged lamely. "I just have a feeling, is all."

"Maybe some trace of the guardian lingers for a while?" Garret said. "A . . . scent, or something."

Ellen gave him a withering look. "An active labyrinth is a kind of tightly folded space. It doesn't have a *scent*." She paused, looking reflective. "I suppose there could be some kind of backup power source. That might keep it going for a while, even without a guardian."

"Maybe," Garret said. "But regardless, without a guardian, it's just a harmless set of confusing passageways. All we have to do is find our way through."

"Still," Ellen said. "We should be careful."

"I'm always careful."

Garret addressed the rest of the group. "All right, in we go. Ellen and I out front, Dex bringing up the rear. Stick close together."

"Which way are we going?" Ellen said, eyeing the room inside the tower. There were no other doorways on this level, only the staircase leading up and down.

"Up," Garret declared confidently. "I saw a bridge near the top. We should get as high as possible, it'll be easier to see where we're going."

And a longer fall, Alice thought, but she didn't argue. She hadn't really expected Garret to turn back, and in all honesty she wasn't sure they ought to. *He has a point, after all. Geryon wouldn't have sent me here if it were as dangerous as the Dragon thinks. And Ending would have warned me.* But something about Garret's attitude made her uncomfortable. *He's too . . . confident.* Her own explorations of Geryon's library had taught her to never be too certain of her assumptions.

In single file, the apprentices passed through the doorway and into the tower, giving the pile of books a wide berth. Soranna maintained her place beside Alice, while Isaac stayed as far behind her as he could, huddled inside his trench coat as though he'd much rather be anywhere else. Garret led the way up the stairs, big stone things dished in the middle by centuries of wear, and they began to climb.

The steps were too steep for Alice to ascend comfortably, and her legs were soon burning with the effort. She tugged on Spike's thread for extra strength, and adopted a kind of bounding gait, leaping off each step in turn and bouncing to the next. Dex, following behind, laughed delightedly at the sight, but Soranna was unable to keep up. She looked so miserable that Alice slowed her pace again.

After three floors, passing three more piles of books, they reached a level with a doorway opposite the one they'd come in by. Garret, glancing through, reported that it led to another staircase that wound around the *outside* of the tower and ended in a walkway. He led the way through, and if climbing with a sheer drop on one side bothered him, he gave no sign of it. Alice herself kept one hand flat against the stone wall of the tower, for all the good that would do, and determinedly did not look down.

Now that she had some sense of the scale of the towers, Alice wondered how long it would take them to get to the dome at the center. *It might be miles, even if we could go in a straight line!* She hoped some of the others had brought more in the way of provisions than she had.

At the top of the staircase, just as Garret had said, the path leveled out into a long bridge stretching across to another tower. From this angle, climbing up from underneath, Alice could see there was nothing supporting the thin stone as it crossed the gap, no pillars or buttresses underneath. She supposed it must be held up by magic, but that didn't make her feel much better, especially once she remembered that Esau's spells would be coming undone now that he was dead. *It doesn't seem like a very sensible method of construction to me.*

Garret apparently didn't share her misgivings. He started out across the bridge without waiting for the others. Isaac followed, and Alice was hurrying to catch up when someone behind her started screaming.

She turned. Dex and Soranna were a few steps down. Beyond them, coming around the curve of the tower, was something very unpleasant indeed. It reminded Alice of an ant, except this creature was as big as a horse. Four glittering, multifaceted eyes topped a black round head, above a pair of pinching mandibles as long as Alice's arm.

Eight multijointed legs moved it along with a constant *click-click* of chitinous armor. It was too broad to use the stairway, but it didn't need to. The thing clung to the side of the tower like an ordinary ant scrambling up a kitchen cabinet, as though the law of gravity simply didn't apply. The rearmost of its three body segments ended in a long tail that curled back over its head, tipped with another pair of pincers.

Dex ran up the stairs as fast as her legs would carry her. She reached the screaming Soranna and gave her a shove to get her moving.

"Run!" Dex shouted. "Across the bridge!"

Garret's head appeared over the edge of the stone

walkway. "What is going—" At the sight of the thing, he swore. "Get behind me! I'll handle this."

"No!" Dex said, reaching a level with Alice. *"Run!"*

Alice had been pulling on her threads: the Swarm for protection and Spike to give her the strength to rip the ant-thing off the tower. As Dex passed her, though, she saw the head of another of the ant-things emerge around the curve of the tower, then another. There was a whole herd of them in pursuit. She heard Garret swear again.

"Keep going!" he shouted. "Get across!"

Dex hustled Soranna up onto the bridge, and Alice backpedaled up the last few steps just as the ant-thing reached them. Its tail whipped forward, and Alice ducked, the pincers *clack*ing over her head. It lunged at her again, but she sidestepped and gave it a shove with all of Spike's strength. The thing staggered, but its rear legs remained stuck to the tower.

More ants were swarming over the stairway and clinging to the tower wall. Alice backed onto the bridge, and risked a glance over her shoulder. Dex and Soranna had not yet caught up to Ellen and Isaac, who were almost halfway across the bridge. Garret had turned back, darkness gathering around his hands like black smoke.

Another ant-thing reared up in front of her, tail swiping. This time Alice avoided the pincers and got her hands around the tail itself, hauling back and yanking the creature off its feet. All eight legs writhed as it tried to right itself, but she didn't give it a chance to get up. Swinging it by the tail like a rock on a string, she gave it a mighty heave off the edge of the bridge and watched it fall twisting into the abyss.

Garret came up beside her as more creatures climbed onto the bridge, clinging to the sides like ants crossing a stick.

"Go on," he said. "Catch up with the others."

"I can help—"

"I'll handle it," Garret said. As Alice watched, he slashed one hand through the air, and a thin curtain of shadow struck the leading creature and sliced clean through it. The two twitching halves collapsed on the walkway, oozing something black and vile, and slowly slid over the side. But the other creatures continued their advance. Garret raised his hands in front of his face, like a boxer, and barked a laugh.

Alice, after a moment's hesitation, kept running. Horrible sounds came from behind her, the *cracks* of breaking chitin and the soft *whoosh* of slashing shadow blades,

mixed with Garret's taunts. She had almost caught up with Dex and Soranna when a sharp *click-clack* of armor-plated limbs warned her that something had gone wrong.

Two ant-things had gotten in front of them, bypassing Garret by climbing along the underside of the bridge. The two girls stumbled to a halt, and Dex ducked nimbly under a lashing tail, but Soranna wasn't quite so agile. A pair of pincers closed around her waist, seizing her in an iron grip and lifting her completely off the ground. She gave a high, piercing wail.

"Soranna!" Alice shouted.

She ran toward the creature, but was blocked by another ant-thing. Alice grabbed its pincers, holding them apart with all the force of Spike's strength. Ahead, another creature had cornered Dex, who was slashing at it with two swords that shimmered like silvery moonlight. The monster holding Soranna was retreating with its prize, back over the side of the bridge.

"Garret!" Alice shouted, hands trembling with the effort of keeping the ant-thing's pincers apart. "Do something!"

"What?"

Garret turned, saw Soranna disappearing over the edge of the bridge, and moved fast, sending out a wave of shadow that cut the creature in half. The front part crashed to the stone, but the rear, already half over the edge of the bridge, wobbled drunkenly on collapsing legs. Then, tail still clutching Soranna, it toppled and started to fall.

Time seemed to slow down, the girl's terrified scream telescoping into a thin whine. Alice didn't waste her breath with shouting. She ducked from between the ant-thing's mandibles, letting them snap closed where her head had been, and ran for the edge of the bridge. At the same time, she dug in her pocket and pulled out one of the three acorns. As Soranna went over the edge, Alice tossed the acorn to the ground, pulled on the tree-sprite's thread with all the mental strength she could muster, and jumped.

CHAPTER NINE
FREEFALL

THE ACORN SPROUTED AS soon as her power touched it, like a wound-up jack-in-the-box released at last. White-green tendrils surged in all directions, growing with manic speed. One of them caught up with Alice as she jumped, wrapping around her ankle and growing along with her as she fell.

Below her, Soranna was struggling free of the pincers of the dead ant-thing. Alice pressed her arms in and made herself as narrow as possible, like a diver, until she was close enough to the girl to grab her arm. Alice pulled her away from the creature and into a tight embrace, then closed her eyes and sent her attention back up the slender thread of root.

As they fell, fast-growing tendrils sprouted in the other direction, scrabbling for purchase between the tight-packed stones. Tiny blind rootlets pushed their way into the cracks, desperately digging in. Alice made the root holding her ankle slow its growth and begin to thicken, taking up the strain of her weight. *But slowly. Slowly!* Too much would snap it. *And even the Swarm isn't going to save us from this fall. Tough skin or no, we'd just be a smear on the rocks . . .*

She banished the thought and concentrated. Her descent began to slow, but she could feel the fibers of the newborn tree groaning in protest. Up at the top, where it held on to the bridge, the roots started to slip and tear free. Alice's stomach lurched. *It's not going to hold!* She tightened her grip on Soranna. *Come on, come on!* The long root creaked. *Almost there—*

All movement stopped. Alice cautiously opened one eye.

She and Soranna hung from the end of the root, twisting gently in the soft wind. Below, there was only the darkness of the bottomless abyss. Alice could feel the root still growing, twining its way between the rocks to solidify its hold, but something else had kept it from breaking free, right at the end. Holding Soranna carefully, she looked upward. Far above, a face was visible over the edge of the bridge, holding on to the root with both hands. It was too small to make out features, but the poof of hair was unmistakable. *Dex.*

Alice let out a long breath and looked down at Soranna. The girl was no longer screaming; in fact, she'd fainted, lolling in Alice's arms like a dead weight. *And, under the circumstances, I can't say that I blame her.*

Even with Spike's strength, she couldn't climb the vine while holding on to Soranna. Instead, she directed it to grow around them both and pull them up. This was a slow process, as the energy she'd stuffed into the acorn was beginning to run out, and by the time they had made it back to the edge of the bridge the fight was over. Ant-things scattered in pieces across the path. Dex helped her up, and between the two of them they managed to lift Soranna back onto solid ground. Garret slung the unconscious girl over his shoulders, and they hurried across the bridge to the next tower, where Isaac and Ellen were waiting.

"Come on. This is exactly what we were expecting. Something got loose from a book, that's all."

"I have to disagree, Brother Garret. What are the

chances such a creature would attack us at the first tower we reach? This was a deliberate ambush."

"Then those things were placed here before Esau died, and they haven't wandered off yet. It's still no reason to panic."

They were sitting cross-legged in a small circle, trying to decide what to do next. The heart-stopping terror of the fall was slowly unfreezing in Alice's chest, giving way to a bubbling anger.

"No reason to *panic*?" she said. "Soranna could have *died*."

"We'll have to take better care of her," Garret said, glancing at where Soranna lay stretched out on the floor. "I don't know what she's doing here, to be honest. She's too young for a job like this."

"This was *supposed* to be simple," Alice said.

"Dex is right," Isaac said. "That was a deliberate ambush."

The others all turned to him, startled. Alice didn't think he'd said more than three words on the whole journey thus far. Now he shifted uncomfortably in the depths of his tattered trench coat. "That was just the first tower. If the wards have disappeared, are we going to run into something like *that* on every bridge?"

"I can handle it," Garret insisted. "We wouldn't have

been in any danger there if we'd stayed in a proper group."

Ellen, uncharacteristically quiet, had been sitting with her chin in her hands while her halo flickered gently overhead. She suddenly got to her feet, glancing down at the still-unconscious Soranna and then over to Garret.

"Come with me for a minute," she said to him. "We need to talk."

Dex sighed and leaned back on her elbows as the two older apprentices circled the mound of books on the floor until they were out of sight.

"What are they doing?" Alice said.

"Deciding," Dex said. "Brother Garret and Sister Ellen will confer and do as they think best."

"That doesn't seem fair. Don't the rest of us get a choice?"

"Only whether to follow or return home," Dex said. "Unless you wish to strike out on your own."

Alice looked over at Isaac for support, but he was gone, slouching off in the other direction with his coat flapping behind him. *What is* wrong *with him, anyway?* Alice took a deep breath, fighting her exasperation. She shuffled over to Soranna to make sure she was still breathing comfortably, then looked up at Dex.

"I don't think I've thanked you," Alice said. "For grabbing the root when I went over."

Dex smiled ruefully. "I am not certain my small weight contributed much to the rescue. But when I saw what you were doing, I could not simply stand idle."

"It's more than Garret did," Alice said. "He was going to let Soranna fall!"

"Do not be too hard on Brother Garret," Dex said. "I imagine he had a great deal on his mind at the time. And not every master gives his apprentices the education that yours has."

Alice sat up a little straighter. "I'm not sure what you mean."

"The True Way, as the Most Favored instructed me, teaches that everyone who bears the great gift is sacred and precious. If it had been in my power, I would have done as you did. But some of the masters misguidedly teach their apprentices that others of their kind are to be regarded as rivals. Enemies. They would not weep at a reduction in their number."

"What?" Alice looked down at the sleeping Soranna. "That's crazy. She's just a little kid."

"She is not much younger than you, I think. I do not know her story, but I am afraid it is not a happy one." She shook her head. "Brother Garret may be correct in one respect, however. I am not sure she should be here with us."

There was a moment of silence. Alice swallowed, and ventured, "What about Isaac? Do you know him at all?"

Dex shook her head. "I have not had the privilege of working with Brother Isaac, but he seems to know you—"

Soranna moaned, and Dex hurried to her side, digging a canteen out of a pocket in her robe.

There's an easier way to answer that question. Alice left Dex to care for Soranna and went in search of Isaac. He hadn't gone far. She spotted him sitting halfway up the stairs to the next floor, huddled under his ratty greatcoat. As she approached, he looked up at her briefly, then hung his head again. It was hard to tell in the torchlight, but she thought that his eyes looked red. *Has he been crying?*

"Are you all right?" he said, after a long pause. His voice was dull.

"Fine," Alice said.

"Good." He lapsed into silence again, letting it stretch on and on until Alice shifted uncomfortably.

"Are *you*?" When he didn't answer, she shook her head. "Honestly, Isaac, what's wrong with you? I thought that after what we went through, you and I were . . ." Friends? *A friend wouldn't have stolen the book.*

He said nothing. Alice ground her teeth.

"Look," she said eventually. "If you're afraid that I'm

angry with you, then you shouldn't worry. Not that I don't have a *reason* to be angry, and I reserve the right to be angry at a future date, but I think we have to get through this first. Don't you?"

"Alice . . ."

"Yes?" It sounded too eager, and Alice cursed herself for letting excitement run away with her.

"Please don't talk to me anymore."

"What?"

She was stunned. Before she could recover, Garret was calling their names from below. Isaac got to his feet and slouched past her, refusing to meet her eye.

Alice followed Isaac down the stairs, fuming, and found all the others gathered round. Soranna was sitting up, and was accepting a few swallows of water from Dex's canteen. Garret was smiling, but Ellen still wore her characteristic scowl.

"How is she?" Garret said to Dex.

"Awake," Dex said. "I do not believe she was badly injured, but she has had a considerable shock."

"I'm fine," Soranna said. Her voice was soft and trembling.

"Okay." Garret clapped his hands. "We're going on, at

least for now. But we're going to take more precautions.
I'll take the lead, Ellen will bring up the rear, and we'll
stay close. No more ambushes like last time."

"Wait." Alice bristled. "Why do you get to make the
decision?"

Ellen rolled her eyes. "If you don't feel up to it, you're
welcome to go home by yourself." She looked at Isaac.
"That goes for you too. Though you're on your own
explaining things to your masters."

"What about Soranna?" Alice said. "One of us could
take her back to the portal—"

"No," Soranna said, faintly but distinctly. "I will stay
with you."

Garret laughed. "At least she's showing some spirit."
Alice glared daggers at him, which he ignored. "There's
a bridge two floors up from here that leads closer to the
center dome. If Sora can walk, we'll get started."

"Soranna," Soranna muttered, but Garret was already
turning away.

Alice and Dex helped Soranna to her feet. The girl was
a little wobbly at first, and Alice remained by her side as
Garret led the way up the spiral stair around the tower.
Isaac followed Ellen, still refusing to meet Alice's eye.

"You saved me," Soranna said, after a while. "But why?"

"Why what?"

"Why would you do that? Risk yourself for me? I'm . . ." She gestured down at herself, then shook her head.

"I don't . . ." Alice didn't know what to say. *What does she mean*, why? When someone was in trouble, you helped them, if you possibly could. "I couldn't have just let you fall."

"You could have."

Alice shrugged uncomfortably. "I'm sure you would do the same for me."

"No," Soranna said. "I wouldn't."

She walked ahead, leaving Alice staring after her.

CHAPTER TEN

THE COILS OF THE LABYRINTH

SISTER ALICE! BEHIND YOU!"

A long, mottled green-and-purple tentacle with razor-edged suction cups slid up over the side over the bridge. It waved back and forth for a moment, as though tasting the air, then snaked in her direction.

Alice felt like a car with only fumes in the gas tank. She'd never pushed her magical abilities this hard for this long, not even against the Dragon. This was the seventh or eighth bridge they'd crossed—she'd lost count—and practically every step of the way had been contested by monsters. It was like walking through a zoo where all the cages had opened, and the lions and bears were free to snack on the guests. Except that Alice would have welcomed a good, honest lion at this point, compared to the menagerie of weird insectoid and crustacean creatures that had attacked them.

For what felt like the hundredth time that day, she reached for her threads.

Dex, on the other side of the bridge, was fending off a similar tentacle with her paired swords. Ahead, the octopus creature had heaved its body onto the thin stone walkway, *clack*ing a bright orange beak. Isaac directed a storm of sleet and ice into its eyes and Ellen sent bolts of blinding energy into the tentacles as they came into view.

As usual, it was Garret who really turned the battle in their favor. As Isaac froze the creature in place, the older boy slowly and methodically slashed the thing to pieces. Its mucus-wet hide was too thick for his shadow-waves to leave more than long cuts, so he concentrated on the tentacles, severing them one by one. The octopus-thing gave a curious groaning bellow, severed stumps spouting an awful green fluid, and dragged itself back under the bridge with its surviving limbs.

The next tower was only a few hundred feet away.

Without discussion, the six apprentices ran toward it. Alice paused to grab Soranna's hand, though her legs felt like lead weights and her feet screamed with pain at every step. She practically cried out with relief as they made it through the doorway and into the now-familiar circular room with its central mound of books. Alice lowered herself to the ground, shaking, and Dex sat down beside her. Soranna simply collapsed into a heap against the pile of books, eyes closed and breathing hard.

Even Garret's eyes were bright with exhaustion, but he remained on his feet, stalking around the pile of books.

"There should be another bridge off this level that leads straight to the dome. I could see it from the outside," he said. "As long as we keep going . . . Oh."

He stopped. Alice roused herself enough to peer over the mound of books, and saw him standing on the other side of the room, staring at unbroken wall.

"Wonderful," Ellen said. "I thought we climbed to the roof of that last tower so you could see where we were going."

"We did. And I *did* see where we were going."

"Evidently not." She let out a heartfelt sigh. "I suppose that means another climb."

"I know this is the right way to the center," Garret

insisted. "The next bridge is just a level or two up or down, that's all. I'll find it."

"Brother Garret," Dex said. "We need to rest. Perhaps afterward I could help to find the way?"

"I've got this under control." He frowned. "And I don't want to stay here any longer than we have to."

"I'm not sure I can cross another bridge," Dex said.

"She's right," Ellen said. "And we're getting sloppier. If we keep pushing, somebody is going to get badly hurt."

"All right, all *right*," Garret said. "I'll see if I can find the next bridge. The rest of you just ... wait here, all right? This should be safe enough. Don't wander off."

"I'm coming with you," Ellen said.

Garret seemed too tired even to argue. The two teenagers mounted the stairs leading to the next level up. Isaac, who had been lurking by the doorway, circled around the mound of books until he was out of view and then *thumped* to the ground. Dex shifted to a cross-legged position, hands resting in her lap, and closed her eyes. Soranna looked as though she was already asleep.

Alice, in spite of her weariness, reached out for her threads. Her grip closed around the black line linking her to the Dragon.

You can hear me. I know you can.

There was a long, empty silence. Then, with a sigh, the Dragon's mental voice answered.

I can hear you. But you are deep within the labyrinth now.

We should be only a little ways from the keep, Alice thought. *It's changing around us, isn't it? That's why Garret is getting lost.*

Yes. The connections of a labyrinth are under the control of its guardian. He shifts it to bring you into conflict with the resident creatures.

We're holding our own so far.

Alice was honest enough to admit, to herself, that Garret and Ellen had been holding up more than their weight in that respect. Her initial irritation at Garret's arrogance had faded a little as the extent of his power became obvious. His shadow-waves were accurate and deadly, and his magical strength seemed to be limitless.

He is toying with you, the Dragon said. *If he wanted to destroy you, it would be simple.*

You say "he." Do you know who the guardian is?

I believe so. The Dragon hesitated. *He is a labyrinthine named Torment. A cruel, vicious creature.*

So what do I do now? Garret and Ellen won't turn back until we've found Jacob.

I do not know. It's possible you may be able to save yourself, if Torment is distracted by the others.

I'm not going to just leave them.

Then you will die. The Dragon's voice vanished abruptly.

"Fat lot of good you are," Alice muttered. She leaned back against the pile of books, which shifted slightly under her weight. A small volume with one cover torn off slithered down and bumped against the back of her head.

I'll figure something out, she told herself. There was a gnawing, jittery feeling in the pit of her stomach that she couldn't banish, no matter how she tried. *Ashes told me we were going to die when we fell into the Swarm book. And Isaac said the same thing when we fought the Dragon. We'll get through this too.*

Somehow . . .

Alice opened her eyes.

She hadn't intended to sleep, but exhaustion had crept up on her. There was no indication of how long it had been—the night sky visible out the doorway was the same, and the flickering torches still burned at intervals around the walls. Her legs ached abominably, with the bone-deep feeling that warns of aches to come. Nevertheless, she struggled to her feet, causing another small landslide of books.

Dex and Soranna were both asleep too. The others were nowhere to be seen. Alice circled the book-pile, in case Isaac had nodded off on the other side, but there was no sign of him. She looked at the spiral staircase, sighed, and started to climb.

I have to try and convince them. One more time. Even Garret must see that we can't keep this up forever. And if she happened to find Isaac dozing off, then she could pin him down and demand to know why he was avoiding her. *This is getting ridiculous. Could I have done something to upset him? He was the one who trapped me with the Siren song and stole the Dragon's book!*

There was no one on the next level or the one after that. Alice shook her head and kept climbing, trying to force some life into her aching thighs.

On the next floor—just below the roof, she judged— she heard the quiet sound of breathing under the low crackle of the torches. Thinking it might be Isaac, Alice padded around the ubiquitous mound of books as quietly as she could.

Instead she found Garret, leaning back against the pile with his head tipped back and his nose in the air. He looked so silly Alice almost giggled. His cloak flared out to one side, and it took her a moment to realize that it was Ellen underneath it, pressed up tight against him. Her head rested lightly on his shoulder, and his hand was snugged around her waist.

Cheeks turning beet red, Alice retreated as quietly as she had come, back to the stairway. She shook her head. *I could have sworn she couldn't stand him. They do nothing but argue.* It was, she thought, a very odd way to behave.

Having come so far, she decided to climb one more flight, and take a look at the castle from the top of the tower. The steps led up to a circular roof surrounded by an iron railing. To one side, the central dome loomed, surrounded by towers and their wild web of bridges and looking as far away as ever. There was still no sign of Isaac.

What happened to him? Something was badly wrong, she could feel it. She wanted to track him down, to grab him and *make* him tell her what it was, but her pride wouldn't allow it. *Why should I go running after* him? The image of Garret and Ellen cuddling together on the level below sprang to mind, unbidden, and Alice felt herself blushing again. She turned away from the stairs and grabbed the railing, the smooth metal cold under her fingers. *It's not like that at all.*

She stood there for some time, staring out at the castle without really seeing it. When she finally turned around, fingers stiff from gripping the railing too tightly, she discovered she was no longer alone on the platform.

"You don't know how hard it is."

There was a boy standing there. He was taller than Alice, but so thin, he was painful to look at, as though he hadn't eaten for days. His brown hair was a ratty mess, and his cheeks were sallow and sunken, giving his face the look of a skull. Blue eyes stared out at her from deep, dark sockets.

Beside him there was another shape that Alice could hardly make out. It was inky black, not the glossy, furry black of a black cat but black like a hole cut out of the world. She could only tell it was there at all by its silhouette against the stars, until it turned its head toward her. Then a few details became visible—long ivory fangs, yellowed and sharp at the points, and a broad, canine tongue the color of old blood. Above them was a pair of eyes, as blue white as river ice, the pupils huge circles in the dim light.

It was a dog—*not a dog,* Alice thought, *a wolf*—the size

of a horse. In the depths of its gaze she felt a frightening intelligence, and she was forcibly reminded of the first time she'd met Ending, staring into her yellow cat-slitted eyes in the shadows of the library.

Chapter Eleven
TORMENT

THE BOY SHOWED NO awareness of the wolf at his shoulder. He gave Alice a hesitant smile, and waved one hand weakly.

"Hi," he said. "We thought . . . *I* thought . . . we'd have a visit. You know. Talk about things. We don't think . . ." He trailed off, as though he'd lost his place, and shook his head. "I'm not sure. It's hard to remember. What's your name?"

"Alice," said Alice, doing her best not to stare past the boy at the huge figure of the wolf. "But who are you?"

"I'm . . . I'm Ev—" He stopped, and his brow furrowed, as though with considerable mental effort. "Jacob. I'm Jacob."

"Jacob." Alice's eyes went wide. "You're Esau's apprentice?"

"Yes. Or I was. Until I killed him." Jacob gave a sad little giggle.

"But we've come to find you!" Alice said. "You can come back with us. We'll all get out of here."

"I'd like—" Jacob stopped, eyes bulging. His throat worked, as if he were choking.

"You've come here to kill him, you mean," said another, much deeper voice. The wolf padded forward a step. It was big enough to look down at Alice. "Or drag him to your masters, which amounts to the same thing."

"I . . ." Alice couldn't exactly deny that. "If you can explain, it might help."

"I didn't want to do it," Jacob said with sudden vehemence. "I couldn't help it. I didn't have a choice—"

"That's about enough out of you," the wolf interrupted. Jacob stopped speaking immediately, as if he'd been gagged. "I apologize for his gibbering. Do you know who I am, girl?"

Jacob's eyes were desperate and pleading. Alice looked away from him with an effort to stare up at the wolf.

"I can guess," she said. "You're Torment. Esau's labyrinthine, the guardian of this labyrinth."

"I see my sister Ending has explained a bit," Torment said. "She's also told me a good deal about you. I wanted to get a look at you in the flesh."

Alice drew herself up a little taller and took a deep breath. "If she's told you so much about me, she must have mentioned that my name is Alice, not girl. And I don't appreciate being stared at like a zoo exhibit."

Torment chuckled, a deep, wet sound. "I see she was not exaggerating about you."

"Now that you've gotten your look, what do you want with us? Are you going to keep leading us around in circles?"

"It *has* been amusing, I must say. Your struggle is pointless, but you're so persistent. I would love to drag this out for days. How long would you keep trying? Until there were four of you left? Three? Two?" He leaned closer, until Alice could feel the hot wind of his breath. His eyes were huge, blue-fringed pools. "One? All alone in the dark?"

"That's *not* going to happen."

He chuckled again. "I can smell your fear, girl. Don't worry. You're perfectly safe. As for the others, it's past time I disposed of them. A pity to end things so soon, but, as you humans say, needs must."

"I'm not going to let you hurt them," Alice said. Her voice rose. "I'm not!"

"No?" Torment said. "This is my labyrinth. Here am I everywhere and nowhere. I am the walls, the stairs, the floors, and the sky." His voice rose to a thunderous roar, so loud that Alice had to clap her hands over her ears and squeeze her eyes shut. *"Who are you, Reader, to* let *me do anything?!"*

When she opened her eyes, Torment and Jacob were gone. Alice, ears still ringing, ran for the stairs, only to find that Garret and Ellen weren't where she'd left them. She kept running, taking the steps two at a time, but when she reached the level on which they'd come in, there was no sign of Dex or Soranna. Isaac was nowhere to be seen.

Alice stared around wildly. The pile of books looked different, she was sure of it. She circled it at a run, but couldn't find the spot where she'd slept. It was hard to tell after running in circles on the staircases, but she thought the doorway was in a different position too.

It's not the same tower. Her mind filled with panic. *He* moved *me. And now—*

She turned around and raced back up the steps, fighting a vicious stitch in her side. By the time she got back to the roof, she was panting for breath, but she flung herself against the rail and looked down for any signs of the other apprentices.

They could be anywhere. In her mind, she could still hear the echoes of Torment's awful laugh. *One? All alone in the dark?*

There! A light bloomed, far below, and Alice recognized the piercing beam of Ellen's halo amidst a small group of hurrying figures. They were running from a tower doorway onto a long bridge—being *chased* out, Alice saw, by a swarm of flapping, bat-like things. The creatures circled the light in a vast shoal, swinging toward it in unison, only to be driven away by a burst of brilliant energy from Ellen or waves of shadow from Garret. Beside the two teenagers, the other three apprentices ran hunched over, shielding their faces from the swarm of fliers.

Alice looked down at the bridges radiating out from the tower she was standing on and did a rapid calculation. None of them would lead her directly to the others, but one would pass over them. From the right spot, a sufficiently insane person could jump, and hope very hard to be on target . . .

Not much choice. Alice ran back down the stairs until she found the right doorway, and sprinted out onto the bridge. Below her, the small creatures attacking the apprentices had been joined by a pack of much larger things. The little ones turned out to be *fish*, not bats, with broad, sail-like fins. The bigger creatures were more like dolphins, but with a green sac where the dorsal fin ought to have been. They maneuvered agilely through the air with their flippers. When one of them darted toward the apprentices, Alice saw it bare a mouth full of nasty teeth. Dex ducked and it sailed just over her head. Garret caught the next one with a shadow-wave, and it fell screeching past the bridge and into the darkness.

They'll be all right. Alice slowed her headlong run, trotting along the side of her own bridge to keep the battle in view. She was trying to gauge the point at which she should jump—the fall would be forty or fifty feet, which ought to be all right if she hardened herself with the Swarm. Unless, of course, she missed the bridge entirely, in which case it wouldn't matter how tough her skin was. *Maybe this isn't such a good idea after all.*

Something *moaned*, a vast, terrifying sound that echoed off the rocky spires and seemed to come from a hundred directions at once. Everyone below froze, looking around for the source of the noise, while the attacking creatures scattered in all directions like startled minnows. Alice was close enough now to hear Ellen shouting and to follow her pointing finger, down into the darkness.

An enormous, bloated thing rose out of the darkness, lit by its own pale green illumination. It looked like a deformed, rotting whale, covered with huge, scabby lumps. Five stalks protruded from its forehead, like the antennae on a slug, and as all five aimed down at the apprentices, Alice realized those must be its eyes. Enormous, fleshy lips peeled back from interlocking triangular teeth like the blade of a hacksaw. Its tail flipped lazily, propelling it above the bridge and then down toward the apprentices.

"Get out of the way," Alice heard Garret yell.

"But—" Ellen began. He shoved her aside.

"Go. Now!"

Even from her high perch, Alice could feel the tension as he pulled hard on his threads. Shadows raced toward Garret from all directions, wrapping his body in shivering darkness. Waves of shadow, like rippling black ink, fell all around him, until he became a black splotch against the torchlit stone. Then he unfolded into a humanoid figure, twice the height of a man, shreds of blackness swarming and boiling around it.

The thing Garret had become stepped into the air, as though climbing an invisible staircase, moving to intercept the whale-thing descending like a falling mountain of tumorous flesh. He raised one hand, palm up, then closed it into a fist. A puff of inky smoke shot outward and wrapped the whale-thing completely in dark mists. The pale green lights vanished, and Alice's heart leaped.

He did it! He—

The pall of black smoke shivered. The shadow-creature cocked its head, as if curious.

Then the bulk of the whale-thing hurtled out of the cloud. A huge wound on its flank trailed a streamer of blue-black blood, but that didn't seem to slow it down. Its mouth opened, yawning wider and wider until its whole head had levered itself apart, the ring of teeth forming a perfect circle, like the jaws of a bear trap.

Garret raised his hands, but too late. The whale-thing was already on top of him, and its jaws snapped closed with unbelievable speed, as though they really were a bear trap and Garret had taken the bait. Teeth met with a *clack* like a gunshot, and Garret was simply gone, vanished inside the creature's huge bulk as if he were no more than a passing fly.

Alice heard Ellen scream. The whale-thing descended toward the bridge, plummeting almost straight down, its broad tail lashing wildly. The apprentices ran in both directions, sprinting for the relative safety of the towers at either end of the span.

"Isaac!" Alice's shout was lost in the *crunch* and *clatter* as the creature hit the bridge. Huge blocks of stone groaned and fell away. It tore away a section fifty feet wide, and the surviving ends began to crumble, unable to support their own weight. A billowing cloud of pulverized rock kept her from seeing what became of the others, aside from glimpses of shrouded figures running for dear life.

She was so focused on trying to see what was happening below that she didn't see the whale-thing's tail coming until it was too late. It snapped up and slammed against the bridge she was standing on with colossal force. The impact threw Alice into the air and clear of the walkway entirely, with nothing beneath her but empty space. Too stunned even to scream, she could only close her eyes as the endless fall began.

Chapter Twelve
INVITATION

Alice hit a flat stone floor, but not very hard, as though she'd accidentally rolled out of bed. She lay absolutely still for a moment, spread-eagled on her back, her breath coming shallow and quick and her heart hammering like it might explode. In her mind she heard the *clack* of the monster's teeth coming together as it swallowed Garret, over and over, followed by the *crunch* of stone as the bridge came apart while she stood watching, frozen and helpless.

Isaac and the others had already been running. They might have made it.

She opened her eyes. The stars looked down at her,

brilliant, distant, and uncaring. The dark, torchlit bulk of several towers loomed nearby.

So I'm still in Esau's fortress. She'd entertained a wild hope that she might wake up at home in bed; after all, that was what had happened the last time she'd nearly died, fighting the tree-sprite. *But this is different.* That had been a prison-book, and Geryon had been watching over her shoulder. Here, inside another Reader's labyrinth, there was no way for the old wizard to even know she needed help.

I wish Ashes were here. The cat was never much practical use, but having him around was comforting nonetheless. *Or Ending. Or even Isaac.* That brought her full circle, though, to her last glimpse of scurrying figures on the collapsing bridge. *I'm sure they made it. They had to.* Except for Garret, who'd been directly in the monster's path. Alice swallowed hard and blinked away tears.

If Ashes were here, he'd tell me to get up and start doing something about it. Alice sat up, rubbing at an ache in her shoulder where it had hit the stones, and looked around.

She was on another stone walkway. But if the bridges between the outer towers had been garden paths, this was more like a downtown high street, broad enough for two cars to drive side by side. Smaller spurs peeled off on both sides, stretching out to nearby towers and weaving above and below each other like a knitter's nightmare.

And straight ahead was the dome of the central keep, lit by its ring of torches.

Okay. Torment must have brought me here. But why?

Alice fingered the pair of acorns that remained in her pocket. All around her was stillness, except for flickers of light from the endless torches. No monsters seemed to be in evidence. It was, she decided, as good a place as any to catch her breath.

Part of her burned to go rushing to the aid of Isaac and the others. But another, more logical part, pointed out that she didn't know which direction to rush *toward*, and running through the labyrinth at random was not likely to help.

It had been hours since her last meal, and she'd had only a couple of swallows from Dex's canteen in the meantime. *Let's hope this works.*

She flicked the acorn to the ground, bent over to put her finger on it, and pulled on the tree-sprite thread. The life-energy packed inside the little seed burst out, sending roots burrowing through the cracks between the stones and branches shooting upward like waterspouts. Alice grabbed hold of the torrent and controlled it, carefully, leveling out the tree's growth when it was five or six feet high and pushing it in a new direction.

Before long, a small, leafy tree stood incongruously in the middle of the bleak stone path. Alice, one hand on its trunk, watched hungrily as green buds formed on its branches, swelling rapidly into small, round fruit hanging from thick stems. It was a little odd, she reflected, to get fruit from what was after all an oak seed, but the power of the tree-sprite overrode any petty biological limitations. It was merely a matter of directing the life-force she'd packed into the acorn along the proper channels.

Two dozen of the fruits were ready, turning a bright orange-red as they ripened in seconds. Alice picked one and took a cautious bite. It was almost like an apple, but not exactly. It was sweet, though, and so juicy it practically exploded in her mouth. She rapidly munched it down to the stem and reached for another.

A few minutes later, satisfied, she picked the remaining fruit and stuffed them in her pockets. The tree's leafy branches, relieved of this weight, rustled in the breeze.

Alice felt a pang of sympathy for the plant—conjured by magic into the hostile environment, it wouldn't survive for long—and shook her head as she sat down with her back to the trunk. *Now is not the time to get sentimental.*

She let her mental grip fall on the black thread at the back of her mind, winding beneath the others. The Dragon.

As soon as she touched it, she felt an odd tension thrilling through the dark strand. Somewhere, another mind was reaching out for it, and there was only one person that could be. *Isaac! He's alive.* The knot of worry in her chest loosened slightly, and she had to remind herself that she was angry with him. *Besides, we're not out of danger by a long way.*

She directed her thoughts toward the Dragon itself.

I know you think it was foolish of me to come here. You're probably right. But I am here, and I need your help, or else I really am going to die. Please.

There was a long silence.

I am listening, the Dragon said. **But I may not be as much help as you imagine.**

There is no way you can you talk to Isaac?

No. As I said, he is . . . closed to me.

Alice frowned. *Do you have any idea why Torment would bring me here?*

This appears to be the front entrance to the keep. I would surmise that he is offering you an invitation.

But why? Why me and not any of the others?

I don't know.

I think you're lying. Alice clenched her jaw, waiting for a roar of rage, but it never came. Instead there was a pause, so long she worried that the Dragon had stopped speaking to her entirely.

Then, a hint of steel in its rumbling mental voice, it said, **Why do you say that?**

Because I think you're one of them. Alice took a deep breath. *A labyrinthine. You can sense the labyrinth, and Ending called you her brother. When Torment called her his sister, I thought—*

I see. Very logical.

Is it true?

. . . yes. We are kin.

So do you think Torment singled me out because of my bond with you?

Perhaps.

In that case, Isaac would probably be safe as well.

Alice's fear eased a little more. *Isn't there anything you can do to help? Can you . . . fight him, or show me the way out of here?*

I cannot.

Alice drew herself up tighter against the tree trunk. *Is it because I'm not strong enough to use your power?*

It has nothing to do with you. The matter is between myself and my siblings, and I am under no obligation to explain it. Suffice to say I cannot intervene. I have said too much already.

A spark of anger surfaced in Alice's mind. *Then it doesn't matter to you if we all die?*

I do not believe Torment means to kill you. Indeed, he saved your life when you fell from the bridge. As for the others, they are not my concern.

I suppose you'll still be safe in your book.

As you would be safe in a prison cell. The Dragon's mental voice became a snarl. **Spend a thousand years locked in irons before you presume to lecture me.**

Then it was gone. Alice breathed out and relaxed her grip on the thread, leaning her head back against the rough bark.

An invitation. She stared down the broad avenue at the dome. *I'm supposed to just follow along?* At the bridge she'd been reduced to a bystander. Now she was apparently to be a passenger following along a set of rails.

She got to her feet, dusted herself off, and gave the dome a vicious glare. *All right. You asked for it.*

A few minutes later, a distant scream drifted across Esau's fortress. Alice stopped in her tracks, straining to listen, but it wasn't repeated. It had been a girl's voice, though, and as far as she knew, there were only three human girls in the fortress at the moment.

The domed keep was just ahead, but Alice turned away from it and ran in the direction of the voice. She followed it down a narrow, curving bridge that arched through the night air for a considerable distance before ending in another tower, pausing every so often to listen. Another scream, louder, told her she was at least headed in the right direction.

She reached the end of the bridge, and the tower loomed ahead of her. She could see another bridge, two stories up, so she ducked through the archway and up the familiar spiral staircase, two steps at a time. The doorway out was right where she expected, and she ran through to find herself—

—back on the avenue, near where she'd begun. The

domed keep rose up in front of her. Her little fruit tree, already wilting slightly, was the only landmark on the endless walkway.

Torment. Alice gritted her teeth. There was another scream, distant now, and she started running again, down a curving bridge that turned into a helical staircase. She descended for what felt like an age, but when she neared the bottom, she saw that it joined up with the same broad avenue, just where she'd started. Alice growled and turned around, running *up* the stairs at a dangerous speed, but after a single turn around the spiral, she stumbled out onto the flat stones in front of her tree, panting for breath.

Labyrinth. For the first time, she really understood what that meant. She thought of Vespidian, who'd fled from her into the dark reaches of the library, and felt a sliver of pity for the vile little sprite. She pictured Ending playing with him, like a cat with a half-dead mouse. *Except now,* I'm *the mouse.*

The keep was ahead of her, once again, closer than ever.

He is *playing with me,* Alice realized. If he wanted her to go to the keep, he could have simply sent her there. *He's made that clear enough.* The labyrinthine wanted her to give *up*, to acknowledge his power and go there of her own accord. To surrender.

This is my labyrinth. Here am I everywhere and nowhere. I am the walls, the stairs, the floors, and the sky. Who are you, Reader, to let me do anything?!

"I won't do it!" Alice kicked the wilting tree in frustration. Somewhere, close by, Isaac and the others were in danger, but she couldn't get to them, couldn't do anything to help.

A low sound drifted through the air. Alice recognized Torment's soft, wet chuckle. She wanted to scream. She set off at a run, not caring that she didn't know where she was going, down one walkway and up another. A stairway led up, and she took it, but when she saw it was bringing her back to the keep, she jumped off to land on a nearby bridge between two towers. Her boot slipped, and for a moment she teetered on the brink, arms windmilling wildly, before she managed to push herself forward and fall painfully hard against the unforgiving stones of the walkway.

"I won't do it," she said, tasting blood from a split lip. Another scream drifted across the fortress. "I won't."

She sat up, shaking, and was unsurprised to find that the bridge now led directly to the keep. Alice turned resolutely away from it. Ahead of her was another tower, but there was no doorway, just a blank wall of solid stone. Alice, her body humming with rage and frustration, ran straight at it with an angry shout. She braced for a painful impact.

Instead something shifted, deep inside her. It strained, twisted, and broke with a crack, like one of her bones had suddenly given way. But there was no pain, only a profound sense of space all around, as if she'd been wearing blinders and heavy earmuffs all her life and they'd suddenly been removed. She was still running, and she could feel the texture of the world, like sheer fabric sliding through her fingers, and feel where it was twisted, bunched, and folded over.

The screaming came from over *there*. A long way off. But it was just a matter of grabbing hold of the cloth, pulling it into a new shape, bringing here and there together so they were not so far apart after all. And then—

Chapter Thirteen
THE GRASPING TOWER

ALICE SKIDDED TO A halt. She was still on a bridge, but not the same bridge. The towers rising around her were different. The dome of the keep was nowhere to be seen. Ahead of her, where a blank wall had been, there was an arched doorway into a tower. The scream had come from inside.

She had no idea what had just happened, but there was no time to waste. Alice grabbed the Swarm thread, just in case, and hurried inside. There were no torches on the walls here, and she hurriedly yanked at the devil-fish thread as well to light her way. As the pale green glow revealed her surroundings, she stopped dead, staring around in horror.

The interior of the tower was not like the others at all. There were no *floors,* just empty space. The entire tower was one giant cylindrical room, with a rusty iron staircase winding perilously around the edges.

As her eyes adjusted, Alice could see what looked like tiny, iron-barred windows, though no windows had been visible from outside. When she looked up, she could just see a ball of dull crimson light hovering three or four stories above her. The devilfish light and the hellish glow made for twisting, lurid shadows.

The screams had definitely been coming from above. She began to climb, quickly at first and then more cautiously as the iron steps shifted and squeaked in their bolts. She reached the first of the little iron windows, but nothing was visible on the other side except a darkness so black the devilfish's glow could not penetrate it.

As she passed by, something *moved* behind the bars, pushing through the narrow space and reaching out for her. It was an arm, thin and sickly looking, with grubby skin and long, filthy nails broken into splinters at the ends. The fingers groped blindly, trying to get a hold of Alice, and the nails scrabbled at her sleeve. Alice very nearly took a step backward to get away from the thing, only remembering just in time that "backward" was off the stairs and over a long drop. Instead she batted the thing away and hurried onward.

More arms were emerging from their tiny fixtures, like horrible insects coming out of their cocoons. They came in every variety and skin color, men, women, and small, pathetic children. It was as if an army of prisoners were locked away on the other side of the wall, blind and mute but desperate to grab whatever they could. Alice pushed them aside where she had to, tearing out of their grip whenever they clawed for a hold. They grabbed at her clothes, her pouches, her hair; broken fingernails left long scratches on the back of her hands, and she pulled the Swarm thread more tightly to harden her skin. The temperature rose as she went, as if she were climbing inside a giant oven, and her face was soon sheathed in sweat.

When she came level with the sullen red globe, she could see a small rectangular shape hanging suspended inside, turning slowly as if dangling from invisible wires. It was a book; all of a sudden she understood where she was. It was a piece of another world that had leaked out of a book, like the jungle in Geryon's library. Esau clearly used his towers like Geryon used clusters of shelves. *But what's inside that book, if this is what leaks through?* Alice decided she didn't ever want to find out.

A few more turns of the staircase, dodging eager claws all the while, and she saw that she was nearing the roof. An opening at the top of the stairs showed a circle of blessedly cool and distant sky. Alice ducked under a huge, hairy arm that looked like it belonged to a circus strongman, sprinted the last few steps, and emerged onto the broad circular roof in time to hear another shrill scream.

It was answered by a new sound, an awful wet grinding, like someone crushing a raw steak in a vise. When Alice raised her hand to shed the devilfish's light on what was happening, she let out an involuntary shriek of surprise.

The thing reminded her of a spider, but she would have welcomed a spider, even a giant one, in preference to this. Its body was a round globe of pallid, eyeless flesh, nearly invisible in the midst of a tangle of limbs. These were arms, dozens of human arms, horribly elongated and twisted into unnatural shapes so that their palms served as the thing's feet. More arms rose above them, longer than Alice was tall and with three or four elbows each, reaching out above the "legs" to catch and grab. Like the arms in the window, these were all *different*, thick-fingered men's hands, delicate young ladies', even the waving, misshapen fist of an infant.

The edge of the tower roof was lined by a tall, spike-topped iron fence, and the thing was climbing up it, hauling itself hand over hand. For a moment Alice couldn't see what it was moving toward; then she spotted the thin figure of Soranna, clinging to the *outside* of the fence, crawling desperately bar by bar away from the monster.

"Soranna!" Alice pushed the devilfish's light as bright as it would go and waved, trying to get the creature's attention. It was no good—with its prey in sight, the thing slithered over the top of the fence, heedless of the bleeding rips torn in its lower limbs by the spikes. Soranna took a deep breath, and for a moment Alice thought she was going to jump—

—but instead she pulled herself forward, *through* the bars, like they were no more substantial than mist.

The hands closed on empty air, and Soranna ran toward Alice, gasping for air. The creature spun, pushing itself back over the fence, and landed on the roof. It raced after Soranna, hands slapping the stone with a sound like a hundred people clapping at once.

Alice let go of the Swarm and yanked on Spike's thread, hard enough to bring him snapping into reality. The little dinosaur snorted and then charged, his stumpy legs pumping like pistons. Within a few yards he had accelerated to a gallop, horns leveled at the multi-armed horror. By the time he passed Soranna, Spike's feet were a blur.

Several arms folded down to grab hold of the dinosaur. But Spike was a good deal heavier than he looked, and his charge carried astonishing momentum. One of the monster's hands managed to close around a horn, only to be wrenched around, as though it had tried to grab hold of a freight locomotive. Spike hit the creature like a lead shot put and barely slowed, carrying the big thing backward until they both slammed into the iron fence at the edge of the roof. Metal popped and groaned, and the pair of them might have gone over if the spider-thing hadn't reached out with all available limbs and taken hold of the fence on either side. A whole section of iron rails tilted dangerously outward under the combined weight.

Alice darted forward, grabbing the astonished Soranna by the hand.

"Alice." Soranna blinked. "You came to get—"

"No time. Come on."

"It can climb the tower," Soranna said. "We won't be able to outrun it."

Alice nodded grimly and dragged Soranna to the top of the staircase. She closed her eyes and felt again for that strange, slippery fabric she had grasped, briefly, that had led her to this tower. There was a tension in it, as if someone else were tugging at the other end, but Alice could still grab hold of a tiny section and *pinch*. She felt space twisting around her, and without opening her eyes or letting go of Soranna's hand, she took a blind step forward.

The heat and sullen red light of the tower were gone. When she opened her eyes, the stairway led into a quite different tower, with ordinary stone walls and the usual mound of books in the center of the floor. Alice led Soranna down a few steps, then stopped suddenly as a bolt of phantom pain ripped through her. The spider-thing had lifted Spike into the air, bending the poor dinosaur's limbs in directions they weren't meant to go; Alice hurriedly willed him into nonexistence, and at the same time released the pinch of space. The fabric snapped back, the pathway between *here* and *there* closed, and they were safe.

"You came to get me," Soranna said, in her low, whispery voice.

The two girls had collapsed against the pile of books. Alice wished for a moment that Torment would show himself, so she could laugh in his face and scream defiance. She could feel him pull on the fabric, his distant, ice-blue eyes watching her. *Go ahead and watch. I'll save them all.*

"Alice?"

Alice realized her attention had drifted. She looked over at Soranna. The girl's face was flushed, and there were a few ragged tears in her leather clothes, but she didn't seem seriously injured. Thank goodness.

"Hmm?" Alice said.

"Why?"

"Why what?"

"Why would you come for me?" Soranna drew her knees in, tight against her chest, and wrapped her arms around them. "You helped me before too. I don't understand what you want from me."

"I don't *want* anything," Alice said. "If I hadn't come, you could have died."

"I am a servant of your master's enemy," Soranna said. She rested her chin on her knees. "Therefore I am *your* enemy. My death should make you happy."

"Don't be ridiculous. Even if Geryon and your master aren't . . . friendly, that doesn't mean I would be happy to see you hurt." Alice shook her head. "I don't want anyone to get hurt."

"I don't understand you."

"Aren't you glad we got away?"

"My master sent me here," Soranna said. "If I die, it is because that is his will."

Alice stretched out her aching legs and rubbed her shoulder with one hand, still feeling echoes of Spike's pain. Her elbow bumped against her pocket, and she remembered what she'd put in there. She extracted two almost-apples, took a big bite out of one, and held the other out to Soranna. The girl's face clouded with suspicion, and Alice rolled her eyes.

"Come on," she said. "I'd hardly come to rescue you only to poison you afterward."

Soranna unfolded herself a little and took the apple.

She bit into it, cautiously, and licked up the rich juice.

"It's good," she said softly.

"There's a few more, if you're hungry."

Soranna ate the fruit with small, careful bites, and wiped her mouth on the back of her hand when she was done. She let herself slump back against the books, legs sliding out, and let out a long, shuddering breath. Alice saw tears sparkling at the corners of her eyes.

"I thought . . ." Soranna said, and swallowed hard. "That thing chased me all the way up the tower. With those *hands* grabbing for me. And when I got to the roof, I was sure it was the end. It was my master's will that I die here, and I should have been happy to fulfill it."

"You were screaming," Alice said. "That's how I found you."

"I couldn't help it," Soranna said. "I was scared. I shouldn't have been, but I was. I didn't want to die."

"I have to say that seems normal to me."

"You don't understand."

"No," Alice said. "I don't. But that's okay. We're going to be okay."

Soranna raised her head and looked sidelong at Alice. "I'm not even supposed to be talking to you."

"To me?"

"To any of the other apprentices. My master told me I would be polluted by impure ideas. He said he might be forced to destroy me if I was contaminated."

Alice was about to say that her master sounded perfectly awful, and only stopped herself when she considered that this might be one of the "impure ideas" that could get Soranna in trouble. Instead, she nodded.

"What do you plan to do now?" Soranna asked.

"We have to find the rest," Alice said. "Isaac and the others."

"You think they're still alive?"

"Garret is probably not," Alice said. "But you were, and compared to you, the others seemed like—" She looked for a way to put it delicately. "More experienced fighters."

"I'm not a fighter at all," Soranna said. "I shouldn't be here. If—" She stopped, and shook her head. "Never mind. How do you intend to find them? We got separated after Garret . . . I'm not sure I could retrace my steps."

It's worse than you know. "I may have a way to get to them. I won't know until I try it, though."

"Is it the same way you brought us here?"

Alice nodded.

"An ability of one of your bindlings? I've never seen anything like it."

By "bindlings," Alice assumed the girl meant her bound creatures. She nodded again, cautiously. It was true, more or less, even if the nature of that creature was unusual. *This power to manipulate the labyrinth must belong to the Dragon.* Now that she knew it was a labyrinthine, many things fell into place. It *felt* different than using her other powers, but that could be because the Dragon, an intelligent creature in its own right, was actively granting her its assistance.

What she couldn't figure out was why, or more precisely why *now. If he'd only helped me earlier, I might have been able to get them off that bridge. Garret might still be alive.*

She took up the Dragon's thread, briefly. *I don't suppose you'll answer now, will you?* There was no response, though she hadn't really expected one.

"I'll need to concentrate," Alice said. "And it may take some time. I need you to keep watch here, on my real body, while I go looking."

"But . . ." Soranna looked at Alice, wide-eyed, and then down at her knees.

"What?"

"Why would you trust me to do that?" the girl whispered. "I could easily kill you while you were helpless."

It was such an absurd question, delivered so earnestly, that it was all Alice could do to keep from laughing. She shook her head.

"For the moment," Alice said, "I'll rely on your sense of gratitude."

CHAPTER FOURTEEN

THE SWARMERS GO FORTH

WELL," ALICE SAID. "HERE goes nothing."

She closed her eyes, pulled on the Swarm thread, and seven swarmers popped into being beside her. Alice took a moment to slip behind each pair of eyes and look around to get a feel for how the tower looked from their vantage point, six inches off the ground. Then she sent the first one hopping down the stairs.

Ordinarily, Alice could only send the swarmers out about the length of a football field before they became too difficult to maintain, which wouldn't be useful to locate the others. But Alice had been thinking about the nature of the "fabric" she had folded. Here in the labyrinth, distance was an illusion, a malleable, *changeable* thing in the hands of creatures like Torment and the Dragon. She guessed—hoped, really—it would make a difference.

Well. No percentage in hanging about. Her lip curved in a half smile at her father's favorite phrase. She kept hold of the Swarm thread and reached out for the fabric of space. With a pinch and a twist, she connected the stairway to the bridge outside the tower.

The first swarmer dashed from *here* to *there* without any trouble. She ought to have felt the distance as a weight on their connection, but it was as if the swarmer were only in the next room. *It works!*

The next step was managing all of them at once. She folded another pinch in the fabric and sent a second swarmer through to a *different* bridge, then a third to yet another, until all seven swarmers had left the tower.

Then she started them moving down their respective bridges. At the same time, she shifted her grip on the labyrinth, keeping a portal open just behind each swarmer to maintain the connection to her real body. It was a bit like letting slippery cloth slide through the pinch of her fingers. Alice took a deep breath and sent the swarmers into a run, keeping an eye out for anything human.

Most of Esau's towers were just dumps for books, but here and there were structures dedicated to prison- or portal-books, and those were very strange indeed. One tower was full of water, waves crashing around its doorways with salty ocean spray. Another had been filled from top to bottom by thick, cottony spiderwebs, and Alice hurriedly sent her swarmer running in the other direction before some arachnid decided to have it for a snack. A third tower shone with shifting colored lights, and the happy strains of a vigorous waltz drifted over the nearby bridges.

Alice kept pinching the fabric of space, moving the swarmers deeper and deeper into the fortress, past towers and stairways and endless, crisscrossing bridges. At first she despaired of finding the others—Torment could have scattered them *anywhere* in the near-infinite sprawl of iron and stone.

But Alice began to realize that she could feel something else through the fabric. She could sense *vibrations*, as if a mouse were walking across a tightly stretched cloth. She directed a swarmer toward these vibrations, and finally caught sight of a pair of human figures, two bridges down. It was only a momentary glimpse, but it was enough for her to send all the swarmers rushing in that direction.

That was when she became aware of another presence in the fabric, sliding around her with a grace and power she couldn't hope to match. *Torment.* It was as though the black wolf were sitting beside her, hot breath tickling her ear.

He wrapped his mental grip around hers and started pulling the fold firmly out of her control, like he was prying her fingers apart. One of the swarmers suddenly lost its connection, and the true weight of its distance from her descended on it like a toppling pallet of bricks. It was torn instantly from reality, sending a stab of pain like a silver needle through Alice's heart.

She grit her teeth and urged the others to run faster. Torment was catching up, undoing her folds one by one, and each time a swarmer vanished, the pain increased. Sweat popped out in beads on Alice's face, soaking her hair and running down her cheeks.

Almost there. There were only three swarmers left. Torment pounced on one almost playfully, but the other two were running along the same bridge in opposite directions, racing to reach the two humans Alice could see clearly now in the middle.

Every breath was an effort, but Alice's heart rose as she recognized Isaac and Dex. They were fighting a pair of creatures that were like bats or moths, with four wide, feathery wings, antennae, and a long, curling proboscis. Isaac sent long streamers of ice condensing around its wings, sending it tumbling helplessly past the bridge. Dex had a more difficult time with the other, trying and failing to skewer it with her swords as its flexible tongue lashed out and got a grip on her throat. Before it could tighten, however, Isaac came up from behind, one hand glowing with a power Alice had never seen him use. When he touched the moth-thing's wings, they took flame, and the creature fluttered away wildly before combusting entirely in a brilliant fireball.

Torment ripped the second-to-last swarmer out of Alice's grip. She gave a grunt as though she'd been punched, and tears worked their way through closed eyelids. The last of the swarmers hurried up behind Isaac and Dex, only to find a silvery blade descending toward it. Alice dodged, desperately, and managed to slip aside as Dex's weapon *clanged* off the stone. Isaac, following the movement, caught sight of the swarmer and shouted, "Stop!"

"Brother Isaac?" Dex cocked her head. "What is the matter?"

"That's one of Alice's!" Isaac bent down to grab the swarmer. The little creature's natural instinct was to evade, but Alice clamped down and forced it to sit quietly still while Isaac lifted it and placed it on his open palm, level with his face. Seen through the swarmer's eyes, it was uncomfortably like being picked up by a giant. "Alice? Can you hear me?"

Alice opened her real mouth to reply, paused, and said a rude word. The swarmer couldn't *talk*—its long, sharp beak couldn't handle the sounds of human speech. Hurriedly, she made it waggle its beak up and down vigorously, in a passable imitation of a nod.

"You can?"

She made the swarmer nod again, then hop up and down in irritation. She could feel Torment closing in, and she redoubled her grip on the tenuous connection.

"But this thing can't speak."

The swarmer shook itself rapidly back and forth, like a wet dog. Alice desperately wanted to ask Isaac whether he'd seen Ellen, and if he could find somewhere safe to stay while she came to find him, but all she could do was play twenty questions.

"Are you all right?"

She made the swarmer nod, then hop to the side of Isaac's hand and point at the ground with its beak, looking up at Isaac several times to make sure he got the message. He looked puzzled.

"Down? You're down?" *Shake.*

"Brother Isaac," Dex said, looking over her shoulder. "More of those things are coming. We need to move."

"Stone? Bridge?" *Shakeshakeshake.* "Alice, I don't understand! Ow!"

The swarmer had nipped his arm, drawing a bright bead of blood. It smeared its beak until it was crimson— Alice had to suppress its natural instinct to lick the stuff up—and hopped from his hand back to the ground. There, with Alice's careful direction, it began to paint a message onto the stone.

Torment was trying harder. Alice felt like someone trying to write a note with the wrong hand while a much stronger person pried her hand away from the pen. She managed one letter, two, three, before the blood dried and the swarmer's beak could only scratch impotently at the ground. Isaac was staring.

"S-T-A. Stand? Stab?" He pressed one hand to where it had poked him. "Star?" He blinked as the swarmer went into a paroxysm of shaking.

"Brother Isaac!" Dex said, tugging on his sleeve.

"Stay?" Isaac said. "You want me to stay here!"

Alice made the swarmer nod so violently it almost fell over. Isaac pointed to the tower up ahead.

"We'll be in there. We need to take shelter from these things."

The swarmer nodded again. Alice felt her grip on the fabric slipping.

"But I'll wait for you." Isaac shook his head. "Alice, I'm sorry. I should have—"

Torment peeled Alice's mental grip apart, and the connection vanished. The swarmer was crushed into nonexistence, and Alice gave a full-throated scream as something like a hot poker plunged through her chest.

CHAPTER FIFTEEN
DOWN THE RABBIT HOLE

ALICE! ARE YOU ALL RIGHT?"

"I'm okay," Alice mumbled. Her skin was damp with sweat, and she felt suddenly cold. Her jaw clenched tight, making it hard to talk.

"Can you sit up?"

Alice nodded weakly, and with Soranna's help she levered herself into a sitting position against the pile of books. The world spun wildly around her for a few moments. Soranna produced her little hip flask of water and offered Alice a drink, which she accepted gratefully.

She could feel her muscles beginning to unclench.

"Thank you."

"It's nothing," Soranna said, looking shy. "I ... *owe* you. What happened?"

"I found Isaac," Alice said, handing the flask back. "And Dex. And I *think* I'll be able to find Ellen as well. But Torment caught me."

"Torment?" Soranna looked confused, and Alice remembered she hadn't explained about the labyrinth.

"I'll fill you in later," Alice said. "Right now Dex and Isaac are holed up in a tower, and we need to get over there ourselves. Once we're all together, we may stand a chance of finding Ellen without getting killed." She certainly didn't intend to try the stunt with the swarmers again. It wasn't only phantom pain she felt when the little creatures died or were forcibly banished; some basic part of her, some energy, was being torn away. "Give me a minute, and I'll see if I can find a path."

Soranna nodded. They passed a moment in silence. Alice was content to simply breathe.

"You're very brave," the girl said, after a while. "It caused you so much pain, but you kept going."

"It's not courage so much as stubbornness," Alice said

frankly. Her lips curled back from her teeth in a grim smile. "I don't like to lose."

When Alice felt strong enough to walk, she got to her feet, and reached out again for the strange, slippery fabric of the labyrinth.

Torment was surely watching her now. But—in spite of his boasts—he couldn't be everywhere at once. Once she opened a path, they'd have a moment to slip through before the labyrinthine could interfere.

"Take my hand," Alice said. "And be ready to run when I say."

She put out her hand to Soranna and concentrated. After a moment, when the girl hadn't moved, Alice looked back at her.

"Is something wrong?"

"N . . . no," Soranna said. She held out her hand to Alice, tentatively, like a small bird testing a perch. Alice grabbed her tight by the wrist and grinned at her surprised squeak.

"Okay," Alice said. "Follow me."

She reached out for the fabric of the labyrinth, ignoring a prickle of remembered pain. *The Dragon is letting*

me use this power because it's the only way to get past Tor-
ment. That means I'm the only one who can help the others.
She found the spot where she'd left Isaac, and felt the tiny
vibration that marked his presence in the nearby tower.
A grip and a twist were all it took to bring *here* to *there*.

Torment pounced, his mental grip prying at Alice's
hold, but she was already running up the last few stairs.
Instead of emerging onto the roof of the tower, she and
Soranna stepped up onto a distant bridge. Alice hurriedly
let go of the connection, and she could almost hear Torment's irritated snarl.

Ahead of them was a doorway into a tower. Some sort
of curtain blocked the entrance, a cross-hatched pattern
of twisting green shoots like a spray of weeds. Light
leaked out through the gaps, startlingly bright against
the gloom of the fortress, and Alice guessed this was
another place where a book had leaked into its environment. *Hopefully it's not as horrible as the last one.*

"Isaac said they were going to hide in there. Are you
ready?"

Soranna nodded. Alice stepped forward, one hand
raised to push through the weeds. She felt the rich
softness of soil and plants under her boots, and caught

the nose-tickling scent of grass. Encouraged, she took another step, through the curtain, and promptly fell over.

It was not really her fault. As she passed through the curtain, something very strange happened to *down*, shifting it ninety degrees. Alice, caught by surprise, lost her footing and ended up face-down in the dirt. Fortunately, instead of a stone floor, there was a bed of soft grass to break her fall, and she had just about recovered enough to stand up when Soranna came through, squeaked in surprise, and collapsed on top of her.

Once the two girls had disentangled themselves and gotten on their feet, Alice got a chance to look around the tower. She had seen some strange things in the depths of Geryon's library, but she had to admit that this beat most of them in terms of sheer impossible geometry. By now she was used to spaces much larger than the buildings that contained them, so it wasn't a surprise to find a sun-drenched lawn inside a tower. What was more than a little startling was that the grass was growing—and Alice was standing—on the *walls*. It felt for all the world as though *down* was toward what had been *sideways* the moment before she stepped through the doorway.

The lawn rolled away from her, grass neatly trimmed

to a uniform length and groomed around a few small shrubs. It was like someone had taken a well-maintained park and rolled it into a tube, like a cigar. It was obvious that the direction of *down* changed with the floor, since the shrubs halfway up the curve of the wall stood just as straight as the grass under Alice's feet. She couldn't help following the ground with her eyes, fighting a dizzy sense of vertigo, to where it began to curve back. Directly overhead, a small brook burbled happily through a rocky watercourse, oblivious to the fact that it ought to have been raining directly down on Alice's head.

Alice found herself laughing as she looked about, in spite of the desperation of their circumstances. She wanted to run all the way around until she got to the brook, and look at Soranna standing upside down on the ceiling. She *really* wanted to see what would happen if she threw something high enough to reach the very center of the tube, halfway between the walls. *Which direction would it fall?*

"I think I'm going to be sick," Soranna muttered. She glanced fearfully at the ceiling, with its upside-down stream. "Esau ought to have kept his books under better control. My master would never allow such foolishness."

"We just have to stay long enough to find Isaac and Dex," Alice said. "Come on."

The doorway was easily visible, a rectangular depression in the turf covered by a mat of grassy roots. Satisfied she could find her way out again, she led Soranna across the grass, looking for a landmark.

It didn't take long to find one. In the middle distance, there was a commotion—Alice saw a group of large creatures gathered together, like a herd of sheep. In its midst was a small building, made of neat brown bricks and roofed with wooden shingles. It looked like the groundskeeper's shed on a better class of golf course. As they approached, Alice caught first a chorus of angry honking sounds from the creatures outside, and then, distantly, the faint strains of a melody she recognized.

"That's the Siren," Alice said. "Isaac uses her to put things to sleep. And if he's using her, I think he's in trouble."

"Those things do not look friendly," Soranna said.

Taking a closer look, Alice had to agree. They were about the size of horses, with fat turkey-like bodies covered in dark feathers, a pair of orange, scaly legs ending in big clawed toes, and two long, flexible necks, each ending in a bullet-shaped head with beady black eyes and a long, sharp beak. The neck and head feathers were a riot of green, blue, red, yellow, pink, and every other hue Alice could imagine.

If she'd seen them in a picture, Alice would have found the things beautiful and charming, if a bit silly-looking, but it took only a few moments of watching them to see that they had vicious tempers. Whenever two of them bumped against each other, the closer head on each would lash out with a nasty peck, sending blood and tufts of feathers flying. They honked and squawked constantly, ripping at the turf with their claws. The ground around the shack was already churned to mud. As best as Alice could tell, they were trying to get into the shack, slamming themselves against the brick walls and scraping at the mortar.

"There are more of them on the other side," Alice said. "Let's circle around, I bet there's a door."

Soranna nodded, and they worked their way in a broad circle, staying well clear of the flock. Alice found cover in a small cluster of shrubs about fifty yards away. A few of the birds had looked in her direction—having two heads, they could hardly help it—but they didn't seem to notice her, being fully occupied in feuding with their fellows.

On this side, the flock was much larger, and they were shoving and fighting to get close to a wooden door set into the brick.

Alice could *see* the Siren, floating above the roof of the shack, translucent as a smudge of white smoke in the brilliant, sourceless daylight. The ghostly figure of a woman had her mouth open in continuous song, and Alice could hear a faint backwash of the melody, but its full force was directed down at the bird-things. As she watched, one of the creatures closest to the door wobbled and collapsed, and there were several lying on the ground already. But the Siren couldn't seem to entrance more than a half dozen at once, and each time one of the things fell over, one on the ground would shake itself awake and surge to its feet.

"Isaac is trying to hold them off," Alice said. "But I don't think it's working very well."

The bird-things were considerably hampered by their constant infighting, but they'd already done quite a bit of damage to the door. Splinters flew every time one of them got the chance to rake the wood with its claws.

"If they notice us, we haven't got a chance," Soranna said. "I doubt we can outrun them, and aside from in there, we haven't got anywhere to hide. Can you fight that whole flock?"

Alice shook her head. There had to be sixty or seventy of the big bird-things. "And Isaac doesn't have enough power to put them all to sleep."

"Can you open a path in there?"

"I don't think so." Alice felt for the fabric and tried, but it was somehow too close to rearrange space to her liking. Or maybe there were too many people—creatures—watching; at home in the library, she remembered the bookshelves always did their shifting behind her back. There was still a great deal she didn't understand about the Dragon's power. "It's no good. Have you got anything?"

"Nothing that would be useful against those creatures." Soranna looked down at her hands. "As I said, I am not a . . . a fighter."

But Alice was staring at her thoughtfully. "You did something when that awful creature was coming after you, back on the other tower. I saw you step through a solid iron fence."

Soranna nodded. "The creature is known as the Geist. Summoning it is very difficult, but I can call on its power to pass through objects for a short time."

"How long?"

"A few seconds, usually. A minute at the longest. I have

to hold my breath, since my lungs won't draw in any air while I'm intangible."

"A minute . . ." Alice stared at the honking, squabbling flock. "That might be enough."

"Enough for what?"

"I have an idea . . ."

CHAPTER SIXTEEN
SORANNA'S GAMBIT

Soranna was shaking her head, nearly in tears. "I can't do it."

"Come on," Alice said urgently. "It's not that far!"

"If I trip, or . . . or *anything*, I'll be torn to pieces!"

"You won't! How can you trip when you're intangible?" Alice was actually curious how one could run while intangible, since running relied on one's feet making contact with the ground. But she felt this was not the time to raise that question. "I know it's not the best idea, but it's all I've got right now. I'll be right here if anything goes wrong."

"But we don't need to," Soranna said. "We can just

escape. You can open a path to the exit book, and we can get out of here."

"I'm not leaving while there's anybody left to rescue," Alice said, a bit more sternly than she intended. "I wouldn't have left you."

"But I'm not . . . like you," Soranna said. "If I'd been in your place, I would have left you behind. I'm not . . . brave, or—"

"You can be," Alice insisted. She looked back at the shack, where the door seemed to be on the verge of giving way. "Listen. We don't have much time. If you're not going to help me, I can't make you, but then you'd better start running, because I'm going to have to try something stupid."

Soranna looked back toward the doorway where they'd come in, and for a moment Alice thought she really was going to bolt. Then, glancing back at the shack, she bit her lip.

"All right." Her voice was tiny. "I'll try."

"You'll be fine," Alice said, with more confidence than she felt. "You remember what to tell them?"

Soranna nodded. "To be ready to run in this direction when we see your distraction."

"Right. I'll start a minute or so after you get through."

"Okay." Soranna took a deep breath, stood up, and smiled shakily at Alice. "As you said, 'Here goes nothing.'"

Alice smiled back, and Soranna started jogging across the turf. Watching from the meager protection of the shrubs, Alice found her stomach churning. *What if she really doesn't make it?* Soranna would be out there in the middle of a flock of vicious monsters, and it would be Alice's fault. That thought was so terrifying that Alice nearly spoke up to call the girl back, but it was too late— shouting loud enough to get Soranna's attention would attract the creatures.

She'll be fine. Alice, crouching, dug her fingers into the grass and gripped hard to keep her hands from trembling. *She'll be fine. She has to be.*

Soranna made it within a dozen yards of the flock before the first bird-thing noticed her. One of its heads snapped around, peering in her direction with the air of a nearsighted codger looking for his glasses. It let out a perturbed squawk, and although the shoving match at the door continued, a few of the creatures walked in Soranna's direction, both heads bobbing pigeon-like in an alternating rhythm.

The girl slowed as she approached them, and Alice's

heart flip-flopped. If she turned and fled now, it would be a disaster. The flock would stampede. *Come on. You can do this!* She was less than a hundred feet from the shack. *Come on!*

Soranna took a deep breath and held it, cheeks bulging. Then, just as the first bird-thing came near, she started to run. The creature gave her a tentative jab with its beak, and shrieked with surprise as its head passed right through her, her form rippling around it like thick mist. Soranna darted forward, walking right through the bird-thing, which stumbled backward in confusion. All the nearest creatures went berserk, descending on Soranna in a storm of ripping claws and slashing beaks. Unable to touch her, they ended up slamming into one another, and half the flock dissolved into an enormous melee. Soranna was forgotten as they shoved, pecked, and honked, sometimes so violently that a single creature ended up attacking one of its own heads with the other.

Alice lost track of Soranna in the confusion, and for a heart-stopping moment she thought the girl had tripped after all. Anyone lying in that field would be trampled under a hundred clawed feet, whether the bird-things were trying to do so or not. But, a moment later, she caught sight of Soranna at the entrance to the shack, ghosting through the sleeping bodies of the creatures there and then slipping into the door itself and out of view. Alice let out a long, shaky breath, unclenched her hands, and got to her feet.

She made it. I knew she would make it. There were red marks on her palms from her fingernails. *Now we just have to hope Isaac will listen.* She thought he would. *Isaac is pretty sensible when he's not being an idiot.*

Alice counted to thirty, then dug in her pocket and came up with the last of her special acorns. She reached out for the brown thread that led to the tree-sprite, and gave it a solid tug.

The creature popped into being, a short, elfin thing with smooth skin the color of a freshly budded leaf. Alice handed it the acorn, which it took with the gravity of someone accepting a sacrament. She pointed toward the flock, and echoed the command in her mind. The tree-sprite nodded and hurried out across the turf.

Her count had reached sixty when the little creature stopped at the edge of the flock. It pressed the acorn against the ground, and through the thread Alice could feel the shivering explosion as the life energy inside poured out. Roots slammed through the soil, shouldering the grass aside in their haste, and a thin tree trunk sprouted upward. It thickened rapidly from the bottom up, like a flat fire hose filling out when the pressure is turned on, and blasted upward and outward, maturing in seconds into a mid-sized oak tree with long, leafy branches. The tree-sprite grabbed hold of one branch and let the growth pull it into the canopy. Bark from the tree slid across its tender green skin, flowing like water until it formed a suit of tough, leathery armor tipped with resin-hard claws.

A few of the bird-things, on the edge of their melee, took note of this new intruder and veered off to investigate. Alice let them get close to the tree, honking curiously. Then, with a twitch of its claws where they were buried in the tree trunk, the tree-sprite brought a mighty oak limb around in a sweep that smashed two of the bird-things completely off their feet and sent them tumbling to the turf, whistling and shrieking with surprise and pain.

In one motion, the whole flock turned around and rushed toward this new threat. Chips of wood and bark began to fly as the bird-things attacked the tree with beaks and claws, heedless of the branches that slapped and thrust at them.

Alice left the tree-sprite to handle the fight on its own

and turned her attention to the shack. Only a few creatures remained by the door, just as she'd hoped. *Come on, Isaac. Come on, come on, come on.* At the rate the things were tearing her oak to pieces, the distraction wouldn't last much longer.

As if in answer to Alice's mental urging, the Siren swept down from her perch on the top of the shack and landed directly in front of the door. The two bird-things still waiting there got the full brunt of her song and toppled over like they'd been pole-axed. The door opened, revealing Dex with her arm around Isaac's shoulders. One of her legs was badly hurt, so she could only walk with his assistance. Soranna hurried out behind them, glancing nervously at the flock clustered around the beleaguered tree.

They weren't moving fast enough. Already a couple of the bird-things had noticed them and sheared off. Isaac sent the Siren to intercept them, and they toppled, but the pile of sleeping bodies around the entrance was beginning to stir. *He can't keep them all down.* And in spite of the damage the tree-sprite was inflicting, the flock was going to demolish the oak sooner rather than later. *They need to run.*

Alice yanked hard on the Swarm thread. A dozen of the tiny creatures appeared, then more and still more. The effort left her gasping. She sent them toward Isaac in a unit, flowing over the neat lawn like a living carpet. The Siren intercepted another curious bird-thing, but Isaac's face was going white with strain. One huge limb of the oak was severed and crashed to the ground, where the furious creatures immediately set about reducing it to splinters.

The swarmers reached Isaac and the others. Alice jumped up from her hiding place in the shrubs, cupped her hands around her mouth, and shouted to them.

"Drop her! Drop Dex!"

Isaac looked up, blinking, but thankfully Dex got the idea at once. She said something to Isaac, and he let go of her hand. Dex spread her arms and let herself topple gracefully forward. Alice was there to catch her, positioning the Swarm in her path like a living mattress. A hun-

187

dred tiny legs worked in unison, carrying Dex over the grass at a speed that left Isaac and Soranna hurrying to catch up.

Alice dismissed the tree-sprite, who had retreated to the very tip of the tree trunk while the bird-things chopped it to pieces, and concentrated on the Swarm. In a few moments, Dex was by her side, laughing as if she were on some kind of amusement park ride. Isaac and Soranna were close behind, both panting. Alice couldn't help wrapping her arms around Soranna in a hug, though it made the girl give a startled squeak.

"You did it! I knew you'd make it."

"I didn't..." Soranna was trembling, hands hovering like she didn't know where to put them. "I thought ... they were going to get us."

Alice let go. "Come on. We have to get to the doorway. Dex, are you all right?"

"My leg is wounded, Sister Alice, but the bleeding is under control for the present thanks to Brother Isaac's skillful ministrations," Dex said. "And I must thank you for this most excellent conveyance!"

"Right. Let's go."

Dex laughed delightedly. "Onward, mighty steeds!"

The Swarm, with Dex on top, led the way, with the three

of them running behind. They angled across the curved surface of the tower wall, aiming for the square hole in the turf where Alice had entered. Behind them, there was a crash as the tree toppled among the flock of bird-things, and a few of them started to look up and take note of where their prey was going.

"They're coming after us," Soranna panted.

"I know," Alice managed, through gritted teeth.

Isaac, head lowered grimly, said nothing. The Siren swooped through the air, and one of the bird-things collapsed, but more of them were following now. Alice and the others had a considerable lead, but the huge, bounding strides of the bird-things carried them forward at a terrific pace.

"They're catching up!" Soranna said, looking over her shoulder. She stumbled, and Alice grabbed her arm and dragged her forward to keep her from falling.

"Just run!"

"Faster!" Dex crowed, spreading her arms like she was flying. "Whee!"

The doorway was coming up fast, but the bird-things were closing faster. *We're not going to make it!*

The Siren blinked out of existence. Isaac turned and raised his hands, tattered coat swirling around him.

Tongues of frost shot out from the turf at Isaac's feet and spread across the lawn.

The first of the bird-things, traveling at a full gallop, stepped onto the suddenly icy ground and found its feet sliding from under it. It was moving far too quickly to stop, and collapsed into a heap, both heads squawking madly. The one behind it tried to go around the fallen creature, lost its footing, and tumbled onto its side. The one behind that went for a jump instead, but was unable to get any traction when it landed and went heads over heels. Bird-things collided in a tangle of necks, flying feathers, and angry, snapping beaks. Another melee developed at once, and the rest of the flock plunged in eagerly, all thought of pursuit abandoned.

Isaac swayed on his feet, his eyes unfocused. Alice grabbed him by the back of his trench coat and pulled him into a run. They covered the last few yards to the doorway, which from this side looked like nothing but a hole, and Alice reached out to take hold of Soranna with her other hand. Dex, getting the idea, grabbed Soranna. *The last thing we need is for Torment to send one of us off alone.* She wasn't certain the labyrinthine could separate them if they stayed close together, but . . .

Alice reached out for the fabric, pinching a path between the other side of the doorway and the roof of a distant tower. She felt, just for a moment, the buzzing tension of someone else moving through the labyrinth, and tried to get as close to it as she could. Then she stepped forward, pulling the others with her.

Chapter Seventeen
TOGETHER AGAIN

THEY TUMBLED OUT ONTO the tower roof together, four apprentices and a heap of bouncing swarmers. Alice let go of her thread, and the little creatures vanished with a string of *pops* like firecrackers. Once she was sure everyone had made it, she let go of her hold on the fabric as well before Torment could interfere.

Then she lay back and concentrated on breathing for a while. Overhead, the stars looked down in cold splendor, and torches flickered and crackled nearby. Someone was laughing, but it was a few moments before Alice had the energy to raise her head and discover who. It turned out to be Dex, and Alice rolled over and crawled to where the girl was lying.

"Are you all right?"

"Just surprised, Sister Alice," Dex said, wiping her eyes with the back of her hand. "And a touch lacerated about the shins, but that is only a matter of the flesh. I told Brother Isaac that my auguries hinted we would escape, but even so, your arrival was startling."

Alice looked down Dex's leg and found the wound, now wrapped tightly in a strip of cloth. A little blood had soaked through, but not too much, so Alice guessed it was okay for the moment. *When I get back, I'm going to dig up a book on first aid.* She shuffled over to Soranna, who was sitting up and coughing weakly.

"How did we end up *here*?" Isaac said. "This isn't the way we came in."

"It's a labyrinth," Alice said. "It's hard to explain, but I can control it, a little. I thought we ought to get as far away as we could." She looked down at the stone roof of the tower. "Besides, I think Ellen is nearby."

"How do you know?" Isaac said.

Alice shrugged. "I can . . . feel her. Sort of."

He shot her a sharp glance, but Dex interrupted. "Sister Ellen is alive as well? The news continues to improve! After the bridge collapsed, I feared the worst."

"I *think* so," Alice cautioned. "I don't really know what I'm doing."

"Very few of us can claim that we do, Sister Alice."

Alice shook her head. "Soranna? Are you okay?"

"I believe I am," Soranna said, looking shyly at Isaac and Dex. "Just tired."

"I am amazed you reached us, Sister Soranna," Dex said. "That was very brave."

"I . . ." Soranna swallowed. "Thanks."

"Alice?" Isaac said. "Do you think I could have a word in private?"

"I thought you weren't speaking to me," Alice said.

"That's . . ." He glanced at Soranna and Dex, and gave her a pleading look.

Alice climbed wearily to her feet and walked away from the other two, and Isaac followed.

"Are you planning to explain yourself?" Alice said, lowering her voice to a whisper.

"I'm sorry," Isaac muttered. "It's . . . complicated. Look, this isn't the time, all right?"

"Fine. But you owe me an answer." Alice crossed her arms. "What did you want, then?"

"The way you're doing all this. It's the Dragon, isn't it?"

Alice nodded. "Do you know anything about these labyrinthine?"

"A little bit. My master always said to be wary of them."

"It's Esau's labyrinthine, Torment, who has been trying to kill us."

Isaac frowned. "How do you know?"

"He came to talk to me. Taunt me, I guess. I'm not sure why." Her brow furrowed. "You have the Dragon thread too. The Dragon hasn't said anything to you?"

"Nothing."

"Well, it talked to me. And now it's giving me this power. I don't know why it's helping. Maybe it just wants to keep us alive."

"If so, it has my support." Isaac hesitated. "Did Torment say anything about Jacob?"

"Jacob came to see me as well, actually. Or maybe Torment brought him along, I'm not sure."

"You saw him?" Isaac blurted. "Was he—I mean, what was he like?"

"He seemed . . . addled," Alice said. "I'm not sure he's in his right mind."

"That makes sense. You'd have to be out of your mind to attack your own master, knowing what would happen afterward."

"Yeah." Alice paused. "That was a good trick with the iceling. You probably saved us all."

"Oh. Yeah." Isaac scratched the side of his nose. "The

tree-sprite was good too. And carrying Dex like that. I mean . . ." He paused. "I never said thank you, did I? For coming to get us."

"No," Alice said. "But we've been a bit busy."

"Sorry. And thank you." She thought she could detect a bit of a blush in his cheeks, and felt a touch of heat rising in her own. "I'm glad you found us, Alice."

Alice cleared her throat. "Make sure you thank Soranna too. I don't know how I would have gotten you out without her."

"Of course," he said, and there was a long silence until Isaac shifted uneasily.

"So," he said. "What now?"

"I think Ellen is somewhere below us," Alice said, feeling for the faint buzz through the fabric of the labyrinth. There was a distinct tone that meant *human*, or possibly *intruder*, easy to distinguish from the creatures that belonged. "I'm going to go down and see if I can find her."

"By yourself?"

"Dex can't walk, and you should stay with her. And Soranna . . . she's done a great job, but she's scared. I've got the Dragon's power, so if worst comes to worst I should be able to get away and find you again afterward."

Isaac's expression said he didn't like it, but he couldn't find any fault in her logic.

Alice crept down the tower stairs with the Swarm thread wrapped around her, hardening her skin in case something leaped out at her. Her greatest fear—and the real reason she'd insisted on going alone—was that Torment would try to separate them again. As long as she had the Dragon's gift, she could rejoin the other three, whatever the labyrinthine tried to do.

For the moment, the fabric of the labyrinth seemed free of Torment's touch. Alice descended three levels, walking round and round the wide spiral staircase. The tower contained nothing more than the usual mounds of moldering books. Alice thought she'd done more running in the past few hours than she had in her entire *life* to date, and she tried to ignore the strident protests from her legs. *How long has it been since we got here, anyway?* With no sun overhead, she'd completely lost track of time.

A *thump* brought her mind back to the present, and she slowed as she approached the next level. She could hear footsteps, and then a muffled grunt and another heavy *thump*, as though someone was moving something heavy. White light played across the stones of the land-ing, moving and shifting along with the noises. *That has to be Ellen's halo.* She paused in the doorway, just out of sight. *Better not to sneak up on her.*

"Ellen?" she said. "That's you, isn't it?"

There was a clatter and *thump,* and a brief silence. Ellen's voice was as sharp and strident as Alice remem-bered. "Who's there?"

"It's me, Alice. I've come to get you."

"You—" Ellen paused. "Come out where I can see you."

Alice stepped up onto the landing, hands in the air. Ellen was standing by another doorway, which was blocked by a barricade of books. Her clothes were ragged, covered in small tears and matted with spots of blood. More blood had dried around a cut on her scalp, and her blond hair stuck up in wild spikes. Over her head hov-ered the white light Garret had called her "halo," and her hands glowed with the same brilliance. Alice remem-bered the beams of deadly radiance she'd hurled at the monsters, and swallowed hard.

"It *is* you," Ellen said wonderingly. "I thought . . . some-thing was trying to trick me, or . . ."

"It's all right," Alice said. "Can I put my hands down now?"

Ellen relaxed, and the white glow faded away. Then, to Alice's utter astonishment, the older girl dropped to her knees and began to sob.

Some time later, Ellen wiped her bleary eyes on her sleeve. "Sorry. I'm sorry. It's just . . ."

"It's all right," Alice said.

Alice felt strange, offering comfort to someone so much older than she. Much less someone like Ellen, who had held nothing but cool disdain for her from the beginning. But, Alice thought, Ellen had been lost and alone all this time. *At least I had the Dragon.*

She guided the teenager over to the pile of books and got her to sit against it, then sat down beside her. For a long time, Ellen was unable to speak, and Alice waited, not sure what to do.

"Did you see . . . ?" Ellen hesitated.

"What happened on the bridge?" Alice cleared her throat awkwardly. "I did. And I saw you and Garret, while we were resting. I didn't mean to, I was looking for Isaac."

"Oh." Ellen's cheeks flamed pink. "Nobody was supposed to know about that."

"I won't tell anyone," Alice said, automatically, then wanted to kick herself as Ellen's eyes filled with tears again. The older girl sniffed and fought down the sobs.

"It . . . couldn't have worked out. I knew that. Something was bound to happen, sooner or later. Readers don't have *friends*, much less . . . anything else. But . . ." She swallowed. "I suppose you wouldn't understand."

Alice thought of the way she'd felt when Isaac had refused to speak to her. "I suppose not," she told Ellen, keeping her thought to herself. "Are you all right otherwise? Are you hurt, I mean?"

"Not badly." Ellen touched the cut on her brow. "I got hit by a rock when the bridge fell apart, and I had to fight a few more creatures before I got here."

"You should come with me up to the roof. The others are waiting."

"Others?" Ellen blinked. "You found some of the others?"

"All of them, actually."

"How? I tried looking, but I can't seem to find *anything* in this place. You were right, it must be an active labyrinth. I don't know *how*, but . . ." She caught Alice's expression. "What?"

"Nothing. I can explain, but let's go upstairs first." Alice let out a long breath. "That way I only have to say it all once."

CHAPTER EIGHTEEN
DIFFICULT CHOICES

THEY SAT IN A circle on the flagstones of the tower roof. Alice, Isaac, Soranna, Dex, and Ellen. The other four listened silently while Alice explained as best she could about her encounter with Torment and Jacob, the nature of the power the Dragon had given her, and what she knew of its limitations.

"I can't keep the pathways open for very long," she concluded. "And it seems to work best at a *boundary* of some kind, like a doorway. I really don't know very much about it."

"Nobody does," Dex said. "My master, the Most Favored, has a labyrinthine, but she told me that not even the masters understand how the maze-demons' powers truly function."

"My master said something similar," Ellen said. "This is the first time I've heard of anyone ever binding one either. I thought they were too powerful for that."

Alice shrugged. "It's too powerful for me to use in the normal way, that's for certain. I think I can only use this power because it wants me to."

"The binding isn't supposed to work like that," Ellen said, frowning. "The bound creature isn't supposed to retain any volition when it hasn't been called on."

"We can figure out what's going on with the Dragon later," Isaac said. "For now you should be glad Alice has it."

"Of course I am," Ellen said, glaring at him. "We'd all be dead without her. Now that we've gotten everyone, we should be able to get out of here."

The words hung in the air for a moment.

"Is that what we're doing?" Isaac said. "Leaving?"

"Of course it is," Ellen said. "What, this hasn't been bad enough for you? If we're in an active labyrinth, it's a miracle we've made it this far. Obviously our masters didn't have the whole story when they sent us here, and under the circumstances, the best thing we can do is try to return and report what we've found."

Ellen looked around the circle, searching for support. Soranna wouldn't meet her gaze, and Dex's smiling expression was a mask. Isaac was scowling. Finally, she looked at Alice, and Alice took a deep breath.

"We haven't got everyone," she said. "There's still Jacob."

"Jacob," Ellen deadpanned. "The boy we were sent here to kill."

Out of the corner of her eye, Alice saw Isaac flinch.

Dex said, "We were meant to capture him for judgment."

"Oh, come on," Ellen said. "If you've already killed your own master, you're not going to let a bunch of apprentices drag you away. He has to know what the old Readers would do to him."

"I'm not sure he does," Alice said. "I'm not sure he knows anything. He seemed half mad when I spoke to him, and Torment was . . . controlling him, somehow. I don't think any of this is his fault."

"It doesn't make any difference whose fault it is," Ellen said. "Why should we go back for him?"

"I'm not asking anyone else to come," Alice said.

"Torment doesn't seem to want to hurt me, but that doesn't apply to the rest of you. I'll open a path back to the portal-book for all of you, and then go after Jacob alone."

"Alice." Ellen's expression softened. "I know you feel bad for Jacob, but think about this for a minute. You'll just get killed if you try this by yourself."

Alice swallowed hard, but matched the other girl's gaze levelly. Ellen's halo flickered and danced over her head, like a wavering candle flame.

"I'm going with Alice," Isaac said. "The rest of you can do what you like."

"What?" Ellen said.

"Why?" Alice said.

"Because you're right," Isaac said. "Jacob needs our help."

"But—"

The thing was, Alice hadn't exactly been telling the whole truth. Torment wanted something with her, and she in turn needed something from him. *If anyone knew how Esau was involved in my father's death, it would be his labyrinthine.* If she left now, the old Readers would have no choice but to get involved, and any chance of finding out what she needed to know would be lost.

But they can't come with me. It was one thing to risk her own life to get what she wanted so desperately. *If Isaac comes with me—if he were to get . . . hurt, or anything—*

It didn't bear thinking about. Alice shook her head violently.

"You can't. I mean . . ." She paused. "Look. Torment doesn't want to hurt me, he told me that himself. I'll be fine."

"Right," Isaac drawled, catching Alice's eye. "Because we both know that labyrinthine always tell the truth."

"Brother Isaac is right," Dex said. "You only know that Torment has not harmed you yet. His ultimate intentions are still unknown."

"All the more reason we should *all leave*," Ellen said.

Dex shook her head. "Sister Alice makes a good point. If Brother Jacob is in thrall to this maze-demon, we must help him."

"*You* can't mean to stay," Ellen sputtered. "You can't even walk!"

"I have been speaking to Sister Soranna," Dex said, "and she believes she can help me with that problem."

"You're going along with this as well?" Ellen said to Soranna. The younger girl flinched from the teenager's gaze, eyes firmly on the floor, but she gave a tiny nod.

"No!" Alice blurted. "Listen. I wasn't asking for anyone to help me. I don't want your help!"

"I don't think that's your decision," Isaac said.

"But . . . I can't . . ." Alice shook her head. It was like sending Soranna out to run past the bird-things all over again. *I can't be responsible. Not for everyone.*

"You're all crazy," Ellen said. Her eyes glittered, threatening a return to tears. "Garret was the strongest one here, and he *died.* Don't you get that? If we don't leave now, we are all going to *die.*" She turned to Alice. "You can't let them do this."

Alice looked around the circle, one face at a time, then down at her hands.

"I'm not sure I can stop them," she said in a small voice.

"*Fine,*" Ellen snapped. "Wonderful. Have fun getting killed. Would you mind dropping me off before you go?"

They walked down the stairs, Dex leaning on Isaac, to the first doorway that let onto a bridge. It was easiest, Alice had found, to connect paths to similar spaces—a bridge to a bridge, a stair to a stair.

Alice gestured for the others to turn away and closed

her eyes. It was definitely simpler to fold the fabric of the labyrinth while no one was *looking* at it. She reached out across the fortress, feeling for the long bridge they'd taken to the first tower, and pressed a path into being. When she opened her eyes, the doorway opened onto that bridge, and the small stone platform with the portal-book was only a few hundred yards away.

She touched Ellen on the shoulder. "It's ready."

Ellen looked out at the bridge, then down at Alice. "You're really not coming?"

Alice shook her head.

"You must . . ." Ellen sniffed. "You all must think I'm a terrible coward."

"That's not it at all," Alice said. "I'd *like* to leave. I just can't."

"You're not telling us everything."

Alice said nothing. Ellen shook her head, wiped her eyes one last time, and walked through the doorway without another look back.

Torment was already closing in, pulling at Alice's path with all the glee of a boy kicking over someone else's sandcastle. Alice gripped the fabric of the labyrinth as tight as she could. "The rest of you should go too," she said. "I can't hold it open for long."

Isaac snorted and turned away. Alice looked at Dex, and finally at Soranna, who shook her head minutely.

"You were right," the girl said in a whisper. "I . . . owe you."

With a last glance at the portal-book, Alice let the connection slip away. Between blinks, the bridge outside melted into a view of another tower, and Torment's mocking chuckle whispered through the fabric.

Just wait, Alice thought, trying to banish her doubts. *I'm coming to see you. We're* all *coming to see you.*

CHAPTER NINETEEN
A WELCOME RESPITE

Soranna," Alice said. "You told Dex you could do something for her leg?"

Soranna nodded, then looked away shyly. "For everyone. I think we could use a rest."

"I'm not sure we can afford to take the time," Isaac said.

"It won't be a problem."

Soranna wormed one hand under her collar and produced something tiny from a hidden pocket. It gleamed ruby red in the torchlight, and Alice came over to look closer. The little object was a strawberry wrought in crystal and gemstones, no larger than the nail of her pinky.

"My master gave me this years ago. He said I was never

to use it unless . . ." Soranna stopped, and shook her head. "It doesn't matter. We need it now."

Soranna placed the little berry carefully on the ground. Then, in one quick movement, she raised her foot and stomped down on it as hard as she could. The tiny thing broke with a *crunch* of glass, and a wisp of white smoke rose from beneath the sole of Soranna's shoe. It coalesced, gradually, into a milky-white sphere hovering at about head height. It looked no more substantial than mist.

All four of them waited in silence. After a second or two, a voice, as quiet as the sigh of a breeze, said, "Yes?"

"I call on you in the name of the Seventy-third Eddicant," Soranna said. It sounded like something she'd memorized. "The debt lingers still. We demand succor."

There was another pause before the voice replied. "I am old and tired, and this was a foolish bargain. Your Eddicant tricked us. No human should live so long."

Soranna's expression wavered for a moment, but she set her jaw and said, "I demand succor. It is my right."

"Oh, very well." The misty sphere began to grow, until it formed the outline of a doorway, hanging in midair. Only darkness was visible on the other side, as though it were covered by a black velvet curtain. "As we promised, so many centuries ago, so we pay the debt still. You may sojourn in our realm."

Soranna blew out a breath, making the misty shape waver and swirl. She turned back to Alice. "I wasn't sure that was going to work."

"Not that I'm unimpressed," Isaac said, "but how exactly does this help us?"

"Come inside." Soranna held her hands in front of her, as though parting a curtain, and stepped through the door. She did not emerge from the other side.

Alice looked at Isaac. He shrugged, and held out a hand to help Dex up. With his assistance, she hopped through the doorway, and Isaac went through after her. Alice, not sure what to expect, followed close behind.

She felt something pass across her skin, not quite solid, like a thick, dry fog. On the other side, she was greeted by a low, warm light and the sharp smell of spices, with an undercurrent of cooking meat. She could hear fat sizzling over a fire, reminding her how long it had been since that last quasi-apple. Her mouth watered.

As her eyes adjusted to the dimmer light, she found herself standing with the others inside a vast tent made of purple silk, the size of a tennis court. Oil lamps, small brass ones with curved handles right out of the *Arabian*

Nights, hung from the tent poles and provided a friendly glow.

In the center of the tent was a rectangular table, which positively groaned under a mass of food and drink. Tall glass pitchers stood between trays of sliced meat, soft grilled vegetables, and platters of fruit and cheese. Everything looked as though it had been laid out only the moment before they'd stepped through, and steam still rose from a fire-blackened roast that had been carved to reveal its tender pink interior.

"We'll be safe here," Soranna said. "My master said this place isn't a book-world. It's more like a kind of solid mirage."

"It's not real?" Alice said.

"It looks real," Isaac said. He was staring at the roast. "It smells real."

"It's real," Soranna said, "but it only exists in a kind of . . . gap. There's no time here, not real time. When we go back outside, everything will be just the way we left it."

"You're sure?" Isaac said. "I've never heard of a world where *time* works differently."

"That's what my master told me," Soranna said. "And he brought me here once before. It only lasts as long as

the power from the gem can sustain it, which he said would be about eight hours."

"But we can eat while we're here," Alice said. "Nothing strange will happen?"

"I don't think so," Soranna said.

Alice looked at Isaac, who shrugged.

"Good enough for me," he said. And, as if that had been a pre-arranged signal, the four of them attacked the laden table like starving dogs.

After eating their fill, and guzzling cool, sweet water, Alice and Isaac sat beside the table while Soranna attended to Dex's leg. First she unwrapped the bandage and used a whole pitcher of water to wash away the crusty dried filth, revealing a long, nasty gash that drooled a steady stream of fresh blood. Alice had to look away, but Dex stared at it with wide-eyed fascination, as though excited to get a glimpse of her own insides. *After having her arm bitten off, maybe this is small potatoes.*

Once everything was clean, Soranna called on one of her bound creatures, and a pale orange cream began to ooze between her fingers. She applied this to Dex's leg in great dollops, rubbing it gently over the wound. Dex shivered every time another handful was applied, and out of curiosity Alice stuck the end of her pinky in the stuff. It made her skin feel cool and tingly, like she'd dipped it in rubbing alcohol.

While Soranna was retying the bandage, Alice looked back at the depleted table. She hadn't even recognized half the food, but she'd been too hungry to care.

"What are these, do you think?" she said to Isaac.

"Which?" He put one hand over his mouth and belched. Alice made a face.

"These things that look like giant raisins."

"Search me."

"They're dates," Soranna said. "You've never had one?"

"I'm not sure we have them in America." Alice looked back to find Soranna tying off the bandage with an efficient, practiced motion. It looked a lot more professional that Isaac's improvised wrap. "Is this the sort of food you have at home?"

"This is food for the master," Soranna said absently, cleaning her hands on a rag. "At home, we eat what we can catch in the forest." She looked up and fell silent, becoming aware that the other three were staring at her. Suddenly overcome by shyness, she bent her head over Dex's leg again, pretending to fiddle with the bandage.

"Sister Alice," Dex said, "may I ask you a question?"

"Sure."

"Is it true that you only began your studies with Master Geryon a few months ago?"

Alice nodded cautiously. "Why?"

"Where did you live before that?"

"With my family, of course. My father."

"Out in the world?" Soranna interrupted, her voice full of curiosity. "With mortals?"

"Yes," Alice said. She remembered Isaac telling her that he had been taken to live with his master at a very young age, but she had no idea about the others. "I didn't even know I was a Reader until my father died, and I was sent to live with Geryon."

"That must have been quite a shock, discovering that you weren't normal after all," Dex said.

"I suppose it was. Why? When did *you* find out?"

"The Most Favored discovered me by reading the signs and portents attending my birth," Dex said. "She brought me to live in her palace as a very young girl."

"What about your family?"

Dex shrugged. "I do not remember them. The Most Favored assured me they were well compensated, as is the custom in such cases."

"She *bought* you?" Alice couldn't help but think of Vespidian, trying to make her own father an offer. "That's awful!"

"Oh, no. It is the best thing for everyone concerned. After all, if she had not, I would never have known my power. I could have lived my whole life without ever finding my true purpose."

"But . . ." Alice shook her head, glancing at Isaac for support.

He shrugged. "I can't add much," he said. "I've been with my master as long as I can remember."

"None of you had a family of your own?" Alice looked at Soranna, who shook her head.

"My family . . . died," the girl said. "When I was young. My master has been training me ever since."

That threw a temporary pall of silence over the conversation. Dex, ever cheerful, broke the spell.

"Then, Sister Alice, you must have some familiarity with the mortal world."

Alice blinked. "I suppose I must."

"We hear many strange rumors," Dex said. "Is it true that mortals can fly now? I have always discounted that one, myself. How can one fly without magic?"

"You mean fly, like with an airplane?" Alice looked from Dex to Soranna, but both girls gave her blank looks.

"A machine," she said, slowly. "You know. With engines, and propellers. It's made of metal."

After a moment of goggling incomprehension, both girls exploded with questions. They were, Alice discovered, astonishingly ignorant of the modern world. Dex had seen gaslight, and read about horseless carriages, but knew nothing about electricity, telephones, or radio. Soranna was even worse. She boggled at Alice's description of Times Square in Manhattan, and flatly refused to believe in the existence of steamships.

"You can't build a ship out of *metal*," she said, after Alice repeated her description. "Metal's *heavy*. It would *sink*."

Dex, by gentle prodding, encouraged Soranna to tell a little bit about her own upbringing. Alice hardly knew what to expect, but the first thing the little girl said caught her completely off guard.

"I wasn't born on Earth," Soranna said. "My village—we always just called it the village—is on another world. You can only get there through a book that my master keeps hidden."

"Wait a minute," Isaac said. "I never heard of *humans* coming from any world but Earth."

"We didn't come from there, originally." Though she

still wouldn't look up at Isaac, Soranna seemed to be gaining confidence as she told her story. "Many generations ago, my people lived on Earth. There was a great disaster that threatened to destroy us entirely, but my master the Eddicant intervened and offered us a new home. We have served her out of gratitude ever since."

"What's it like?" Alice said. "Living on another world."

"Hard," Soranna said. "We live in the shadow of an ancient forest, and we hunt the beasts that live there for food. They, in turn, hunt us." Soranna paused. "There were twenty-six children in my cohort. I am the last survivor."

That produced a moment of shocked silence.

"But you were born a Reader," Dex said.

"Yes. Every child in the village is tested by the Eddicant for the talent. In my cohort, there were two, myself and my half sister, Kasdeja. That is very rare, and the Eddicant was pleased. She offered a great feast for the entire village." Soranna smiled slightly at the memory, but then her face fell. "My sister and I went to train together, but she was more talented than I by far. Our master intended that we form a complementary pair, one to fight and the other to support her. You can see that the creatures she chose for me to bind were meant for this."

She indicated Dex's leg, now tightly bandaged. "But I was never good enough to accompany Kasdeja on her assignments. Before I was ready, she was killed in battle. Now my master sends me out alone. I think she would just as soon be rid of me, as a failed experiment."

Dear God. Geryon had warned her that not every Reader trained apprentices as "liberally" as he did, but she had never expected a story like this. *And Dex, bought from her family like a loaf of bread. Who knows where Isaac came from either.* She chewed on her lip. *It's inhuman.*

Geryon is a Reader, Ending had whispered. *His magic is based on cruelty and death.* But from the sound of it, Geryon was a veritable saint compared to the rest of the old Readers. *Or is he?* Alice remembered Emma, the girl Geryon had "helped" by relieving her of her Reader talent, who now served at the Library like an automaton. She shivered.

Dex intervened rapidly to change the subject to a discussion of bound creatures and what they were capable of. Alice demonstrated the Swarm and the devilfish, and Isaac explained that since they'd last met, he'd bound a

fire-spirit called a salamander, which could project fire
or let him melt objects between his hands.

Dex's silver swords, she said, belonged to a holy warrior
she called a caryatid. She used another creature that she
called a "moon-sprite" to generate clouds of milky-white
stuff, like solidified moonlight. She could sculpt and spin
it into any form she wanted, as soft as cloth or as strong
as steel. At Alice's prompting, she crafted pillows and
thin sheets for all four of them, fluffy and white and very
faintly glittering, like clouds flecked with silver dust.

Just the sight of the bedding made Alice realize how
tired she was, and the others apparently felt the same way.
Soranna checked Dex's bandage one more time and then
curled up, making a tight ball under her moon-sheet, and
Dex herself stretched out, careful with her injured leg.
Alice found herself yawning, and was just trying to decide
whether or not her stomach would stretch for one more
flaky meat-pastry, when Isaac touched her shoulder.

"Alice." He kept his voice low. "I think it's time for that
answer I owe you."

CHAPTER TWENTY
ISAAC'S CONFESSION

I HAVE TROUBLE BELIEVING WHAT Soranna told us," Alice said as they walked to the other end of the tent.

"I don't," Isaac said grimly. "It makes sense, from the Reader's point of view. Finding new talents before the others get to them has always been a problem. The Eddicant has created a breeding population to draw from that she can keep all to herself. I wouldn't be surprised if she wasn't the only one."

"But it's horrible! She's got those people living in a world full of monsters."

"Maybe she thinks she can breed them in harsh conditions to produce more Readers. Like picking the fastest horses for studs."

"You can't treat people like horses." Alice frowned. "You sound like you agree with what she's doing."

"Of course not. It's horrible. I'm just saying that it makes sense, from her point of view." Isaac shook his head. "The old Readers do what's best for themselves, always. It's a bit like evolution, really. Any of them who weren't smart and nasty enough were killed by the others long ago."

Once they were out of earshot of the others, Alice turned to face Isaac, arms folded.

"All right," she said. "Explain."

"I need to ask you a question first," he said. "What are you really doing here? It can't be just to rescue Jacob."

Alice blinked, taken aback. "I don't see how that is any of your business," she said. "Besides, he needs our help."

"But you didn't want the rest of us to come with you. If you were just trying to rescue someone, you wouldn't act like you were ashamed of what you were doing."

"I just didn't want the rest of you to get hurt. Torment—"

"You can't predict what Torment will do, and you know it. You didn't want us to come because you've got something else in mind."

"It's not like that," Alice said. She paused. "I *am* going

to rescue Jacob. But there's something else too. I didn't want anyone getting hurt just for my sake."

"Oh." Isaac regarded her thoughtfully. "I can believe that. So what is the 'something else'? Some treasure for Geryon?"

"No! If that was it, I would have left with Ellen. This is something . . . personal. And I told you, it's no business of yours!" She glared at him. "What are *you* doing here? I'm sure it's not out of the goodness of your heart."

"I'm here because of my brother," Isaac said.

"Evander?" He'd told Alice the story, back in the library, when he was trying to convince her to let him escape with the Dragon book. They'd grown up together, until Isaac's master had traded Evander to another Reader like he was a milk-cow. "Why? Was he supposed to be on the expedition?"

Isaac gave a bitter chuckle. "Who do you think we came here to find?"

It took Alice a moment to parse that. When she did, her eyes went wide.

"Wait. I thought *Jacob* was Esau's apprentice."

"Esau changed his name," Isaac said. "Like a *pet*."

"You're certain?"

"Of course I'm certain! I told you, we've met a few times since. He would joke about it." Isaac's expression was dark with anger. "I'm not surprised he killed Esau. That monster deserved it."

"But why would your master send you to kill him?"

"Maybe it's a test." Isaac kicked idly at the fabric of the tent. "He wants to be sure I'm loyal enough, or something. Maybe he just forgot all about Evander, or who he traded him to. I wouldn't put it past him."

"So you knew this from the beginning," Alice said. Isaac's sullen behavior and his bloodshot eyes suddenly made a little more sense. "What were you going to do when we found him?"

"I have no idea. Try to help him escape, maybe. Or maybe convince him to come along peacefully and beg for mercy. I couldn't let the rest of you find out. You'd have tried to stop me."

"And that's why you were pretending I didn't exist?" Alice said.

"I'm sorry," he said. "I thought . . . You were the only one who knew the story. I was afraid if I talked to you, I might let something slip, and you'd figure it out. You could have told the others." He scratched his cheek and looked away, embarrassed. "I thought you were still angry with me."

"I ought to be. Angry, I mean. That was a dirty trick you pulled to steal the Dragon."

"I'm sorry," Isaac said again, looking at the floor.

"When I got here, though, all I could think was that it was good to see a familiar face." Alice shook her head. "At least until you started giving me the silent treatment."

"I'm—"

Alice rolled her eyes. "Please stop apologizing."

"Sorry," Isaac muttered, then realized what he'd said and started giggling. The laughter was infectious, and Alice found herself grinning.

"I'm glad I got the chance to tell you," Isaac said. "I wouldn't want you to think I was just . . ."

"Being a jerk?"

"Yeah." He met her eyes. "Especially if that was . . . the last time we saw each other."

There was a long silence. Alice was blushing again, but she couldn't look away. His eyes were brown, she noted inanely, with a ring of green specks. *Pretty eyes.*

Isaac looked down, breaking the spell.

"So what are you going to do now?" she said. "About Jacob. I mean, Evander. Whichever."

"I don't know." His frown returned. "I had only just worked up the nerve to tell you about it."

"If he *is* being controlled by Torment," Alice said, "that might give us a way out of this. Geryon and the others wouldn't need to punish him if it wasn't his fault."

"You don't know them," Isaac said darkly. "But I guess it's possible."

"We could even convince your master to take him back!" Alice felt a surge of excitement. She had been wondering what would happen to Jacob, in the event that they succeeded, and this seemed like the perfect answer. "You can be together again!"

Isaac's face was a mix of hope and his usual black certainty that something would go wrong. He nodded, grudgingly. "If we could do that . . ."

"It'll work. I know it'll work."

"Yeah." He scratched his cheek again. "Listen. I know you have your own reasons for being here—"

"Not this again."

Isaac coughed. "I just wanted to say thank you. For coming to help Jacob, whatever made you do it."

"Oh. Well. Yes." Now it was Alice's turn to feel embarrassed and look away. "I know I told everyone I would do it alone, but I'm glad you stayed to help. It makes things . . . easier."

"Right." Isaac looked back over his shoulder, toward

the others, and cleared his throat loudly. "I suppose we had better get some rest too."

Dex's moon-cloth blankets and pillows were as soft and fine as any down, and the thick carpets were as good as a featherbed. Alice suspected she would have gotten to sleep just as well if it had been a bed of nails, though; the past few hours had left her exhausted and aching. It seemed like no sooner had she put her head down on the pillow than Dex was shaking her awake, but she guessed she'd been asleep for hours.

Actually, she thought as she sat up, *it has* definitely *been a few hours.* In her parched state, she'd guzzled quite a few pitchers of water during the meal. She caught Soranna's eye as the girl began untying Dex's bandages.

"Has this tent got . . ." Alice gestured vaguely, then, at Soranna's obvious incomprehension, finished, ". . . a toilet? Or something?"

"Oh!"

Soranna covered her mouth with one hand and stifled a giggle. She pointed Alice to a discreet alcove, concealed behind a hanging fold of purple silk. By the time Alice emerged, much relieved, the girl had unwound Dex's bandage to reveal a thin, puckered pink scar, vivid against her dusky brown skin. It looked painful, but from Dex's face as she put her weight on the leg, Soranna's magic had done its work well.

"You have my gratitude, Sister Soranna," Dex said. "I don't know that even the Most Favored could have put me back together so adeptly, and she has a great deal of experience at it."

Soranna blushed, but she was obviously pleased. Alice grabbed a few leftover scraps of fruit from the table and gathered everyone by the tent flap. Their time in the pocket-world was nearly up, and everything was beginning to look a bit insubstantial, as though it was preparing to return to the mist out of which it had been formed.

"Remember," Alice said, "stay as close together as you can. I'll do my best to keep Torment from separating us, but he's probably stronger than I am. Hold hands if you need to. Are you ready?"

"Ready," Isaac said. Dex grinned, and Soranna gave a tiny nod.

Alice swept open the tent flap and ducked through, feeling the solid mist passing all around her. The tower room was just as she'd left it, with Ellen's ruined barricade slumping against the wall by the door. The others appeared behind her, and the doorway of mist wavered for a moment and then collapsed.

"I'll try to open a path to the keep," Alice said. "My guess is that's where Torment is keeping Jacob."

"I'm not sure that will be necessary." Isaac pointed to the doorway.

Looking outside, Alice could see that the view had changed. She was once again looking out on the broad avenue ending, far in the distance, at the domed keep's front gate.

An invitation, the Dragon called it. Apparently now the others are included as well. She wasn't sure if this was a positive development or not.

"I don't like it," Isaac said. "Why would he let us just walk up to his front door? It must be a trap."

"It could be," Alice admitted. "But if we're not going to leave, what other choice do we have?"

Isaac grimaced, but said nothing. Alice led the way out onto the bridge, with Dex and Soranna close behind. Isaac brought up the rear, keeping a wary lookout over his shoulder.

CHAPTER TWENTY-ONE
THE GIANT'S PLAYGROUND

THERE!" ISAAC SAID.

Alice followed his pointing finger. Something was moving on a nearby bridge, paralleling their route to the dome. It kept to the shadows, but she got a glimpse of a long, low shape, with dark fur rippling along its flanks. When it turned to look at them, the lantern light made its yellow eyes glow like a pair of headlamps.

"They're definitely following us," Isaac said.

"I have seen them as well," Dex said.

"They're escorts," Alice muttered. "I think they're making sure we don't leave the path."

Alice wished she didn't feel like a fly accepting an invitation from a spider. *Or a rabbit from a wolf.* She grit her teeth. *If it comes to that, we'll show* him *we aren't just a pack of rabbits.*

A pair of enormous stone doors were set into the wall at the end of the avenue. Alice strode out ahead of the others and pushed on one of them, expecting to have to use Spike's power to shift it, but to her surprise the stone moved easily under her hand. The big door swung inward without even a whisper of sound, revealing an enormous chamber beyond.

It was the sort of room that medieval kings had built to impress their subjects, and Alice supposed it must serve much the same purpose here. Everything was on a grand scale, from the rows of massive pillars by the walls to the mountainous staircase at the rear leading up to a curtained doorway. Torches were bracketed to the stone at regular intervals, and their light glittered off gold fittings encrusting every surface: banded around the pillars like the rings of giants, edging the steps, even in elaborate designs inlaid into the smooth, polished floor.

Most decorated of all was the statue, which stood in the middle of the room as a gaudy centerpiece. It went all the way to the ceiling, at least fifty feet overhead, and depicted a huge, muscular, bearded man, wearing only a loincloth, his hands pressed flat against the vaulted ceiling as though he were another pillar. He was made entirely of polished steel, and every curve of his muscles gleamed in the torchlight. Heavy gold chains hung around the man's neck, and bracelets adorned his wrists and ankles, each a broad hoop of gold or silver that Alice could easily have stepped through. His eyes looked directly down at the entrance, and his expression was thoughtful, as though he were deciding whether to crush the insects below under his sandaled feet.

It was all, Alice felt, in extremely bad taste. Her father had told her once, after they'd visited a colleague's over-decorated mansion, that the fancier the display someone felt they had to put on, the more desperately they wanted to impress you. Even her father might have been awed by the sheer amount of precious metal on display here, but Alice had spent enough time in the world of the Readers to realize that wealth in ordinary, human terms meant nothing to them. There was no point to hoarding gold and gems when in some book, somewhere, there was probably a creature that could create them out of thin air.

By his expression, Isaac had similar thoughts, but

Soranna's eyes were wide. For someone who had grown up in a forest, it probably was impressive. Dex had a calculating look on her face, like a thief sizing up a potential haul.

The front door swung shut behind them, as silently as it had opened. Alice led the way across the polished floor, her boots clattering at every step. They were just coming to the feet of the great statue when the curtain at the top of the steps billowed. Alice halted at once, ready to grab her threads.

Jacob emerged and peered down at them, arms folded. He looked dirty and wan, eyes sunk deep in their sockets and hair wild and unkempt. Alice heard the hiss of Isaac's breath beside her.

"What are you doing here?" Jacob said, in a voice that boomed and echoed throughout the chamber. It was nothing like the hesitant, halting tone he'd used the last time he'd spoken to Alice. "I did not give you permission to enter my domain."

"We're here to help you!" Alice called back. Her voice bounced around the room and came back to her in weird, distorted echoes.

"Here to kill me, you mean, at your masters' bidding," Jacob said. When Alice hesitated, he laughed. "I hope

I've already demonstrated the foolishness of making the attempt."

"Torment is using you," Alice said. "Just . . . come down here and talk to us, all right?"

"Don't be an idiot." Jacob raised his hands. "I have taken up my so-called master's mantle. The sooner the other Readers accept that, the better. I should obliterate the lot of you, to make sure they get the message." He cocked his head. "However, I will show mercy. Leave this place and never return, and you may keep your lives."

"I . . ." Alice paused, not sure what to say. Isaac stepped in front of her.

"Evander!" he shouted. "I know it's not really you saying that. You'd never be *this* stupid."

Jacob blinked. It was hard to read his expression at this distance, but he seemed uncertain. His hands fell to his sides.

"I . . . Isaac?" The deep, booming voice was gone. "Is that you?"

"It's me!" Isaac took a step forward.

"You came . . . for me?"

"Of course." There was a hitch in Isaac's voice. "Of course I did."

"I don't . . . I didn't . . ." Jacob took a step closer. "I

didn't want to do it. You can't make me say I did. I just wanted . . . I didn't . . ."

Alice heard a wet, nasty chuckle, right by her ear.

"Oh, *I see*," Torment said. "How sweet."

Alice spun, but there was nothing there. She felt a shiver in the fabric of the labyrinth, and then a shiver in the real world, a tiny tremor running through the stone.

"No!" Jacob boomed. "I will *not* be deceived."

"What?" Isaac looked stunned.

"It's Torment," Alice hissed. "He's controlling him somehow."

"Sister Alice . . ." Dex began hesitantly.

Jacob turned away and stalked back through the curtain, like a monarch dismissing his court.

Isaac went to follow, then looked back at the others.

"What are you waiting for?" he said. "We have to go after him!"

"Of course we do." A bit of grit landed on Alice's cheek, and she brushed it away. "But we can't afford to just rush into whatever Torment has planned for us."

"No," said Torment's disembodied voice. "Please, don't rush. I'm having a wonderful time."

"Sister Alice!" Dex said.

Alice turned. "What?"

A small stone bounced off her shoulder and clattered on the polished floor. Dex pointed up, wordlessly. Alice looked, up and farther up, until she was staring right into the face of the giant statue. His blank, steel-gray eyes were staring right at her. Then, as she watched, he blinked. The fingers of one gigantic hand flexed, tearing away from the ceiling with the *pings* of breaking bolts and the *crunch* of shattered stone. Dust and flakes of rock began to fall in a steady rain.

The statue closed his hand into a fist the size of a motorcar. He jerked his other hand free. Then the floor began to shudder, and one giant foot lifted a few inches into the air with a screech of overstressed metal.

The apprentices stared up at the thing as though mesmerized. It was like watching an avalanche, Alice thought. It was so huge, so heavy, it seemed utterly inevitable. All she could think of was the shadow of those enormous feet falling across her, and the unyielding steel surface coming down—

Soranna proved to be the quickest thinker among them. She managed to open her mouth to scream.

"Run!"

Soranna's shriek shocked them into motion. All at once Alice was running toward the pillars, with the others beside her, as rocks from the ceiling pelted down all around them.

Behind them, the steel giant wrenched one foot free, and began tugging on the other.

"Anyone have any idea what *that* is?" Alice panted. She grabbed instinctively for the Swarm, hardening her skin.

"Some kind of . . . animating . . . spirit!" Isaac said.

"Any idea what to *do*?"

"Get to the pillars!"

"Right!"

Before they reached the line of columns, the giant had his other foot free. His heavy gold bracelets and anklets rattled as he covered half the distance between them in a single enormous step, bulging steel muscles shifting in his exquisitely carved thighs like rippling quicksilver. One huge hand came down, fingers spread.

Isaac pointed as he ran, and freezing wind blasted directly into the giant's face. Shards of ice shattered on his sculpted beard, against his cheeks, even directly in his eyes, but they had as little effect as hailstones against armor plating. Isaac, looking over his shoulder for a moment, lost his footing and nearly stumbled, but Dex grabbed him by the collar and yanked him forward, just before the giant's hand came down with a squeal of metal on stone.

The apprentices ran into the narrow gallery between the columns and the wall. Moments later, the giant collided with the columns like an animal throwing itself against the bars of a cage. He thrust his hand into the gap between two pillars, trying to reach them, but his bulging musculature was too thick and the arm stuck fast. Huge fingers scrabbled just over Alice's head, clanging like bells whenever they bashed against each other.

It was too loud even to shout, but Alice pointed up the row of columns, and they kept running. The giant tugged, but his arm was trapped. Clenching his other hand into a fist, he swung a roundhouse punch at the stone barrier. Metal met rock as though a bomb had gone off, and the pillar vanished in a spreading cloud of pulverized stone.

The giant grabbed the next pillar around the middle, tearing it clean away from floor and ceiling with horrible splintery crunches. Tossing the remains over his shoulder, he reached out for another.

"Now what?" Isaac said. The giant was between them and a dash for either the stairs or the front door, and the line of pillars was rapidly being reduced to rubble.

"I don't *know*," Alice said, trying to think. *He's made of* steel. The Swarmers' beaks would hardly be able to make an impression, and the statue was so heavy she didn't think even Spike's strength could topple it. *I'm out of acorns, and there's nothing here for the tree-sprite to work with.* The thing could crush rock in his bare hands—even if they somehow managed to collapse the ceiling on him, she was unpleasantly certain he would be able to dig his way out. *There has to be* something *I can do!* She tried tugging at the Dragon's thread, in desperation, but the creature seemed no more inclined to help now than before, and they couldn't get to the doorway to escape by a fold in the fabric—

"He is approaching rapidly," Dex said. She held a silver sword in each hand.

"I can see that!" Alice snapped.

"If we scatter," Dex said calmly, "perhaps only one of us will be squashed. The others might escape."

"We have to be able to come up with something better than *that*," Isaac said.

There were only three pillars left between them and the giant. Alice expected to see him grinning in anticipation, but the sculpted face never changed its expression.

"There has to be something," Alice said. "I just need time to think—"

"I'll draw him away," Soranna said.

Alice stared at her.

"Sister Soranna," Dex said. "Are you certain—"

"My master created me to support my partner." She looked up at the giant as he tore away another column. "I'll try to keep his attention as long as I can."

"Soranna—" Alice said.

"Don't argue!"

"I won't." Alice grabbed her shoulder. "Keep him busy, and we'll think of something."

Soranna nodded. As the giant ripped away the second-to-last pillar, she darted out, running between the chunks of falling rock and passing just in front of the huge statue's toes. The giant turned to follow, letting the ruined pillar fall and catching up to the madly scrambling girl in a single stride. He brought his hand down on her in an open-palmed slap, like a man swatting a fly, and the impact resounding through the floor lifted Alice briefly off her feet and shook more dust and chips of rock from the ceiling.

Soranna was gone, and for a long moment Alice couldn't breathe. *Dear God. There'd be nothing left but paste . . .*

Then the girl appeared again, stepping directly out of one of the giant's outstretched fingers and taking off in a different direction. With a metallic screech, the statue moved to follow, turning his back on Alice and the others. Alice let her breath out with a *whoosh*.

"Over to the other side!" she hissed. "Hurry!"

The opposite wall was protected by its own row of pillars, as yet untouched. Alice stumbled into their shadow with Isaac and Dex close on her heels. Across the room, roiling clouds of rock-dust obscured everything except for the giant's head, but his frantic thrashing indicated that Soranna was still leading him on a wild chase.

"She can't keep it up," Alice muttered. "If she misses the timing even once—"

"She is very brave," Dex said.

"We could make it up the stairs." Isaac eyed the big staircase with the curtained doorway at the top. "There's no way that thing would be able to follow us."

"Don't be stupid," Alice said. "We have to *help* her!"

"How? I don't think anything we have will be any good against *that*."

"We didn't have anything that would work against

the Dragon," Alice said, not caring if Dex overheard. "I wasn't about to give up then either."

"But there's *nothing* here. No trees, no water. Just rocks!"

"I know!" Alice furrowed her brow. *Think, think, think.* A ringing crash came from the other side of the room as the giant slammed against the wall. "You said it was an animating spirit. What does that mean?"

"It means he's not a giant steel monster," Isaac said. "He's a real statue, but he's possessed by some kind of incorporeal creature."

"How do we kill it?"

"I have no idea. But damaging the statue isn't going to do it, and I don't think the Siren will help either."

"If damaging the statue doesn't help, what *can* we do?"

Dex cleared her throat. "While Brother Isaac is correct that we may not be able to kill him by damaging the external shell, that doesn't mean it will not *help*. He would be very little threat if we could tear him to pieces."

"Right," Alice said. "*Right.* He's made of solid steel. How can we damage it?"

"I doubt my swords would make much of an impression," Dex said. She looked at Isaac.

He shifted uncomfortably. "The salamander might be able to melt through. If I summon it, it only gets as hot as a cook-fire, but when I use the power myself I can make it much hotter." He shook his head. "But it only works by *touch*. If I try to get close enough to touch that thing, it'll mash me to jam!"

"I don't think he's very bright," Alice said. "The way he came after us . . . I have an idea. Dex, I'm going to need your help . . ."

CHAPTER TWENTY-TWO
ALICE AND GOLIATH

"Soranna!" Alice stood with her hands cupped to her mouth, trying to make herself heard over the rumble of falling stone and the huge booms of the giant's footsteps. "Soranna! Over here, quick!"

For a moment Alice thought the statue had finally caught up to the girl. Then Soranna appeared out of the cloud of dust, moving at a clumsy jog. There was blood on her arm, and she looked tired and in pain. Alice waved her closer, and Soranna broke into a desperate sprint.

Behind her, the giant had heard Alice's shouts. His blank eyes turned toward the two girls in the middle of the room. A single step brought him close enough to swing a hand down toward them, and Alice ran for it alongside Soranna. The great steel fist slammed into the floor just behind them, sending cracks spidering outward through the stone floor.

"Over there!" Alice shouted in Soranna's ear. "Run to the pillars and hide. I'll take it from here!"

"But—"

"Just go!"

Soranna darted for the temporary safety of the line of pillars where Alice, Dex, and Isaac had taken shelter. Alice herself remained in the open, running back toward the door to the outside. The giant followed, but Alice had eyes only for Dex, who was pressed against the wall by the stairs. Dex waved wildly to Alice, who nodded and changed direction. The statue swung after her, back toward the other side of the hall with its fractured, broken columns.

Halfway there, Alice skidded to a halt. She could see Dex running back to where Isaac and Soranna were hiding. Something trailed behind her, a thin line of silver light almost invisible in the dust, and Alice traced it back to where it wrapped around the statue's ankle. *She needs more time. If he takes another step now, he'll just drag her behind him.* Alice swallowed hard as the giant loomed above her. *I hoped I wouldn't have to try this . . .*

The statue raised one fist and brought it whistling down. Alice, judging the timing as best she could, yanked hard on the Swarm thread as the huge mass of metal descended, and felt the now-familiar moment of disorientation as her body dissolved into a bouncing pile of swarmers. They scampered away from where she'd been standing as fast as their legs could carry them, opening out from the oncoming fist like an exploding dandelion puff.

One of them didn't make it—its legs were tangled in the laces of Alice's boots, which remained upright where she'd been standing. *Why do my shoes always stay behind?* Before she could get the swarmer free, the giant's fist slammed down with enough force to crack the stone floor. Boots and swarmer together were mashed flat, and Alice felt a stab of pain as the little creature died. The rest of the Swarm/girl flowed around the giant's hand and reconstituted itself into Alice's body, now barefoot, standing in front of the broken columns just out of the statue's reach.

Dex had made it. Alice saw her between the giant's legs, running around and around the pillars on the other side of the room. Looking up at the giant, Alice put on her cockiest grin and spread her arms.

"Come on!" she shouted. She had no idea if he understood or not, but it couldn't hurt. "You big ugly thing, here I am!"

The statue took a step forward, or tried to. A nearly invisible line of moonlight-stuff ran from the columns at the other end of the room, around the giant's ankle where Dex had left it, and then back to the pillars. For a moment Alice thought that even this wouldn't be enough, that the giant was so strong he would tear all the columns apart, or else that Dex's moonlight strand would break after all. Dex had assured her it was practically indestructible, but . . .

Then the giant leaned forward. His right foot was in the air, straining against the fine threads but unable to move forward, and his balance was gone. Slowly at first, but with the awful force of a toppling mountain, the enormous statue started to fall.

Alice danced backward as he came down, arms out to catch himself on his palms. The weight of the impact drove the statue's hands into the floor in an explosion of flying rock chips and dust, and Alice ducked behind a severed pillar to shield herself. Then, leaning out, she shouted, "Now, Isaac!"

Isaac was already running toward the giant, his hands

glowing red with the power of the salamander. He reached the huge thing's foot, and paused a moment in concentration. The light from his hands went from red to yellow, then to a furious blue white that shone so brightly it made her eyes water. Through the streaming tears, she saw Isaac plunge his hands against the steel of the giant's ankle, which shifted like wax under a hot knife and began to glow with a dull red light of its own. Isaac tore at it, pulling out huge handfuls of molten stuff and flinging them aside. In a few moments he had torn the statue's foot completely away from the leg, and he hurried over to administer the same treatment to the other.

Hurry! Between the scream of metal on stone and the *crack* and *zing* of fragments, Isaac would never hear her, but she willed him to work faster. The giant was pushing himself up, drawing his leg underneath him. Isaac had only gotten halfway through his other ankle when the statue pulled it away from him, leaving him in the middle of a circle of smoking, molten metal. The giant struggled to get his remaining foot underneath him, rising to a crouch—

And, with a metallic *crack* like a cannon shot, the weakened ankle snapped under the strain of the statue's immense weight. The huge thing toppled sideways, hands flailing wildly, and crashed amidst the ruins of the pillars. Alice jogged well clear of its reach, to the base of the stairs, and beckoned the others to join her. Isaac was still surrounded by shimmering waves of heat, and Dex lent her arm to Soranna, who was limping.

"I don't think he's going anywhere now," Alice said, raising her voice to be heard over the clatter as the giant tried to rise again, only to be thwarted by his maimed legs.

"Are you all right?" Isaac said. He shook his hands, spattering the ground at his feet with molten metal, and then stepped carefully aside before letting the salamander's power fade away.

"More or less." The pain of the swarmer's death was fading from Alice's chest, but slowly. "What about you, Soranna?"

"She was cut by flying rock," Dex said. "It needs bandaging."

"Okay." Alice looked at the giant, who was scrabbling mindlessly at the floor in an effort to right himself. "Let's get going."

Alice led the way through the curtained doorway, where they found a long corridor of polished stone. They passed a few doorways leading to other corridors, all dark and silent, before Alice caught the scent of growing things and heard the burble of water from up ahead.

She ducked into the next doorway and found herself in a garden. It was a small room, with black, glassy walls, full of stone planters housing shrubs, flowers, and a central tree so tall its crown scraped the ceiling.

Alice leaned out and beckoned the others. "In here."

A small fountain in one corner fed a wide, shallow pool. Dex helped Soranna to a seat on the side of one of the planters and started examining her leg. She emptied her canteen over the scratches, then underhanded it across the room to Alice, who snatched it out of the air.

"Think the water's good to drink?" Alice said to Isaac.

"Who knows?"

"Well, if I turn into a frog, you'll know to be careful." She frowned, looking around the room. There was only one doorway. "Speaking of which, let's not get trapped in here."

"I'll keep an eye out." Isaac headed back to the doorway, while Alice went over to the fountain.

She cupped her hands and lifted a mouthful of the water, sipping cautiously. It tasted faintly of stone and dust, but seemed safe enough. She waited a few moments for any magical transformations to make themselves felt, and when nothing happened she went ahead and dipped the canteen, watching the bubbles glug up from inside.

Alice nearly dropped it when a familiar nasty, wet chuckle sounded in her ear. She looked over her shoulder, expecting to find the huge black wolf looming over her, but there was nothing there. When she looked back to the water, though, she could see two blue lights shimmering on the rippling surface, like the reflections of a pair of ice-blue eyes.

"I promised my sister I would look after you," Torment said, his voice a whispery growl. "But I must say you're making it very difficult to keep my word."

"Sorry to be difficult," Alice snarled back. "It's a strange way of looking after someone, trying to crush them."

"If you had accepted my invitation to begin with, or even abandoned the labyrinth when you had the chance, you would have been in no danger. I can't be blamed if you insist on wandering into the line of fire." The wolf let out a long-suffering sigh. "However, as you are intent on being unreasonable, I have decided to offer you a bargain. Consider it my capitulation, if you like."

"A bargain?"

"Not so loud, if you please. This is for you to decide."

Alice looked over her shoulder and lowered her voice to a whisper. "What do you want?"

"I need to get you out of here with a minimum of fuss, or my sister will be very angry with me. Therefore, I agree to your terms. The others can go free. You and I will remain behind and have a little chat. I believe you have some . . . questions for me."

Questions? Alice's heart leaped for a moment. *He really does know something!*

"That seems generous to me," Torment went on. "What do you say?"

"What about Jacob?"

"He must remain here. You must see that there is no other place for him now. But I hope that I have demonstrated that I am more than capable of protecting him from the Readers. He'll be perfectly safe."

Alice bit her lip. "Isaac won't like that."

"Isaac won't have a choice. You are the one to whom my sister has gifted her power. The others will go where I send them."

Gifted her power? Alice was confused for a moment, then realized Torment meant her newfound power to twist the fabric of the labyrinth. *He thinks it's a gift from*

Ending. She paused thoughtfully. *He must not know about the Dragon. I suppose Ending wouldn't tell everyone.*

That wasn't the point at issue, though. *What do I do?* She glanced surreptitiously at the others. Dex was winding a bandage around Soranna's leg, while Isaac leaned out of the doorway, keeping watch. *They stayed because I said I was going to help Jacob.* She couldn't give up *now*, just because Torment had waved the answer she wanted in front of her. *They've helped me this far. I owe them.*

But if Torment is telling the truth, this could be my only chance to find out about my father.

"I don't . . ." Alice hesitated. "I don't think I trust you. What's to stop you from hurting the others once I let you take them away? And what's to stop you from lying to me?" She shook her head. "Besides, you've done something awful to Jacob. He deserves the chance to make up his own mind."

"Foolish girl," Torment growled. "I offer you mercy, and you throw it in my face."

"I'm not afraid of you," Alice said. "We've beaten everything you've thrown at us so far."

"You have been lucky, and I have been indulgent. I warn you one last time. If you turn away from me now, all your friends will die in agony, and you will never know the truth. My patience is finished."

"Good," Alice whispered. "So is mine."

She slashed the canteen through the water, shattering the image of the wolf's staring eyes, and turned back to the others.

CHAPTER TWENTY-THREE
TORMENT'S CHILDREN

Are you sure you're all right?" Alice said to Soranna.

"I'm fine," the girl said, stretching her leg to demonstrate. "It was just a scratch, really."

"I'm glad." Alice shook her head. "You were amazing back there."

Soranna looked at the floor, but she was hiding a smile. "I just bought a little time."

"I, also, was impressed with your bravery, Sister Soranna," Dex said.

"I don't mean to bring everyone down," Isaac said, "but do we have any idea where we're going?"

They were walking down the corridor again, although it had turned several times and the doorway to the garden room was no longer in view. Other doorways opened onto corridors or rooms of every description—a smithy, a long row of stables, empty now, a chamber full of row on row of clay pots stoppered with wax seals. By unspoken agreement, the apprentices left all these alone and continued onward.

"I must admit I have lost my sense of direction," Dex said. "This keep is more like a maze than a proper dwelling."

"We're still in the labyrinth," Alice said grimly. "I can feel it."

"Are you certain?" Dex said. "The Most Favored told me that Readers do not generally live in their labyrinths, lest they fall under the power of their own servants."

"I know Geryon doesn't," Alice said. "But we're definitely still in Torment's domain." She concentrated on the fabric in her mind's eye. "It almost feels . . . newer, here. As if the labyrinth *grew* over this place."

"Torment could keep us wandering forever, then," Isaac said.

"He could try," Alice said. "But I don't think he will." Reaching ahead with her newfound senses, she could feel the labyrinthine's subtle touch on the fabric, guiding their steps. But she could also feel the buzz of another human, and unless there was someone else around, that meant Jacob. "It feels like he's bringing us to him."

"That does *not* reassure me," Isaac muttered.

"Be cheered, Brother Isaac," Dex said. "Whatever our fate, at least our quest nears an end. And I believe the auguries to be auspicious."

Alice wished she were so confident. As the red-hot anger she'd felt after Torment's threats faded, it was replaced with misgivings. Challenging a labyrinthine seemed foolhardy. *Even the old Readers are afraid of them.* Her new power, however unusual, didn't seem like it would go a long way toward evening the odds.

Come on, Alice, she told herself. *No jitters, not now.*

They rounded a corner and came to a large doorway hung with layers of silken curtains. She could feel the buzz of Jacob's presence, just beyond.

"This is it," she told the others. "If Torment comes after us, don't hold back."

All three nodded fiercely, even Soranna. A smile came to Alice's lips, unbidden, followed by a flip-flop of her heart when she thought about what might happen. She took a deep breath, pulled aside the curtains, and stepped through.

◆

On the far side of another grand room, slumped across one of the padded armrests of a fantastically carved throne, was Jacob. Around him, the bas-relief walls depicted soldiers, and in front of them were ranks of statues, similarly accoutered, so it looked as though a stone army was marching out of the walls and into three-dimensional reality.

Alice gave the carved men a long look, in case they were about to come to life and attack, but they only stood at motionless attention. She stepped forward, and Jacob raised his head, but the movement was jerky and wrong. It was as though an invisible puppeteer had lifted him by the hair.

"Stop," Jacob said, in a voice now wholly unlike his own. Alice got the impression that someone else was speaking *through* him. "I have stayed my hand thus far, but if you come any farther, I will be forced to destroy you. I am the *master* of this domain." His head jiggled. "The *master*. I am."

Isaac, at Alice's side, clenched his fists. "What has Torment done to him? He's . . ."

Alice put a hand on Isaac's shoulder. "We're here to help you, Jacob," she said. "Just like we said earlier. We know it's not your fault."

"Not my fault." Jacob's voice cracked, and he put

his head in his hands. "It's not. Not my fault. I never wanted this. Never wanted to be. To be master. I just . . . I wanted . . ."

He threw back his head and screamed, slamming his fist against the back of the throne, over and over. Drops of blood flew across the stone where he'd scraped his fingers raw.

"Evander!" Isaac broke away from Alice, running for his brother. She followed a few steps behind him. As they reached the bottom of the dais, Jacob abruptly jerked to his feet. A huge, dark shape materialized out of the shadows behind the throne and casually cuffed the haggard boy with one massive paw. He hit the ground, rolled once, and didn't rise. Torment padded over to him, looking down, then raised his head and fixed his ice-blue eyes on Alice.

"Pathetic," the black wolf rumbled. "I had hoped he would last a good deal longer than this. A tool that doesn't do as it's told is no tool at all."

"Leave him be!" Isaac shouted. He took another step toward the dais, then halted when Torment put one huge paw on Jacob's chest.

"If he's no use to you, then let us have him," Alice said.

"I'm afraid we're long past the time for *bargains*, girl,"

Torment said, his words rising into a growl. "Though you were right, of course. Your friends would have died one way or the other. That was the whole point of this farce, you see. Not that killing the lot of you is any kind of an achievement, but it's a beginning. *Readers*. The world will be better off without you."

"Sister Alice!" Dex called.

Alice looked over her shoulder. Wolves were emerging from among the statues, slinking out of the shadows and into the torchlight. They were long and lithe, smaller than Torment but still twice the size of the biggest dog Alice had ever seen. Their shaggy coats were black, brown, or streaky gray, though none had the utter light-drinking darkness of Torment's ebony fur. At least a dozen of them surrounded Dex and Soranna, and more slipped among the statues to approach Alice and Isaac.

"My children," Torment said. "My pack. I've heard that some of Ending's offspring are nearly as smart as their mother, but I'm afraid in my case we don't breed quite as true. They understand me well enough, though."

A gray wolf stepped in front of Alice, lips curling back from ivory fangs. It growled, low and dangerous. She risked a glance at Isaac, who was still staring fixedly at Torment and Jacob.

"That's enough to make them useful tools," Torment went on. He prodded Jacob's limp body with his paw. "Unlike this one. A useless tool is broken, and a broken tool is fit only to be disposed of." The huge black wolf fixed his ice-blue eyes on Alice. "Something you would do well to keep in mind, girl."

Then, with sudden, violent speed, Torment's jaws snapped downward.

Isaac screamed, an incoherent shriek of rage and pain. Cold wind lashed out from him, and a long, dagger-sharp icicle formed between his hands and lengthened into a spear. His hand thrust out, and the weapon followed the gesture as if it had been launched from a cannon. It embedded itself in Torment's hide just behind his shoulder, biting deep, but against the wolf's bulk, the spear looked like a toy. Torment, steaming muzzle stained red, glanced briefly at Isaac, then dipped his head in Alice's direction.

"Save me this one," he said, loud enough to fill the room. "Kill the rest."

The wolves leaped all at once, but Alice was ready. She had Spike's thread wrapped around her, and as the first beast came close, she repeated the maneuver she had used on the ant-thing, grabbing it by the forepaw and swinging it around like she was in the park playing crack-the-whip. She spun on her heel and let go, and Spike's strength, added to the wolf's momentum, sent the creature cartwheeling head over haunches to collide with the statues ranked on the other side of the room.

Another wolf lunged past her, heading for Isaac, and she grabbed it by the tail and yanked hard, pulling it off its feet and leaving it spread-eagled on the floor. She vaulted over it, planting a foot heavily on its head in passing, and went for Isaac herself. There were three wolves between him and the throne, and another closing in from behind, but he had eyes only for Torment and Jacob.

"Isaac!" Alice shouted. He didn't look around. The wolf behind him was closing in. Alice grabbed one of its back legs and pulled, sending it skidding across the marble tiles.

The three beasts in front of him got ready to leap. Alice yanked harder on Spike's thread, pulling him into the world, and the dinosaur popped into being between Isaac and the wolves. When they jumped, he interposed himself, catching one of the creatures in the belly with his horns. The wolf toppled, whimpering in pain, but the other two fell on Spike, jaws snapping.

Alice reached Isaac and grabbed him by the collar. She could still feel the bitter cold from the iceling thread he held, but he didn't seem to be *doing* anything with it. She jerked him around to face her, and found his eyes staring and unfocused.

"Isaac!" Wolves snapped and growled all around them. "*Isaac!*"

When this failed to produce a response, she shook him

as hard as she could. He blinked, and his eyes focused on her, but all at once they filled with tears.

"He's . . . he . . ." Isaac said.

"I know," Alice said. "And you're going to be dead too, if you don't *do something*."

"I—" Isaac began, but Alice had already let go of him and spun back to the fight. Where Soranna and Dex had been standing, there was a cluster of tangled, angry wolves, and at first Alice thought the two girls were somewhere underneath. Then she saw them stepping *through* the beasts, Soranna's hand gripping Dex's, her face tight with strain. Once they were clear, Soranna staggered, gasping, and Dex spun away, silver blades materializing in her hand. She cut down the first wolf to leap at her, and the others paused, milling behind the body.

Alice didn't intend to give them the chance to regain their courage. Spike was still fighting beside Isaac, but she unwrapped the Swarm from her own body and summoned as many swarmers as she could. Black balls of fur popped into existence around her and tumbled to the ground like fuzzy hailstones, bouncing a few times before righting themselves and gathering into a single, amorphous mass of sharp-beaked bodies. At her command, they flowed toward the pack of wolves from behind, launching themselves at the legs and ankles of the beasts like tiny lancers. Wolves howled and shrieked, and the swarmers' tongues darted out to lick up the blood from their wounds.

From behind her, she heard a *whoomph* like a gaslight igniting, and she felt a sudden wash of heat. She turned to find a vaguely humanoid figure made of a mass of living flame standing between Isaac and the wolves. The salamander reached out a hand and stroked one of the beasts on the flank, and it burst into flames as though it had been soaked in gasoline.

But more wolves were coming, drifting silently through the alleys between the statues. Alice sent Spike charging at one that poked its head out, forcing it to duck quickly back between the stone soldiers.

"Isaac!" Alice shouted. "Back up! We need to make a circle!"

Isaac had his arms spread wide, raining ice down on one pack of wolves while his salamander chased another back, but he looked over his shoulder and gave a quick nod. He started to back up, and Alice had Spike charge the wolves between her and Dex, clearing a brief path through the mass of beasts. Soranna stood back-to-back with Dex, a long spear made of Dex's moon-stuff in her hands, while Dex herself had changed completely. Alice guessed she'd transformed into the caryatid—she looked like a statue, with dark granite skin, silver armor to match her twin swords, and eyes that blazed with light. The wolves kept trying to circle around her blades, but she lashed out whenever they came in range, and several already bore big, ugly cuts.

"Coming up behind you, Dex!" Alice said, not wanting to sneak up on the girl and get a sword in the face for her trouble. She followed her dinosaur, deploying the Swarm to push the wolves long enough that Isaac could come after her.

With all four apprentices in one place, watching each other's backs, the wolves had no way to sneak around. They kept trying, but one after another was sent flying by Spike, torched by the salamander, or slashed by Dex's glittering blades. Even Soranna, with her spear of sharpened moonlight, drove them back with vigorous thrusts. After a few minutes, with many of their number lying dead or bleeding, the wolves backed off, circling round and round but not daring to approach. Alice sent the Swarm at them again, and felt a fierce joy as a whole section of the pack broke and fled rather than face the onslaught of tiny needles. She grinned, baring her teeth, and turned to face the dais.

"Well?" she asked the black wolf. "Is this the best you can do?"

CHAPTER TWENTY-FOUR
THE HUNT BEGINS

TORMENT'S TONGUE, HUGE AND red, licked Jacob's blood from around his muzzle. He padded forward, stepping from dais to floor without breaking stride. Muscles slid and rippled under his furry flanks like liquid darkness.

"No," he growled. "It is not."

He came on at a walk, stepping across the bodies of fallen wolves, huge eyes never leaving his prey.

Alice nudged Isaac and nodded at Torment. "Together?"

"Together," Isaac agreed, with gritted teeth.

The salamander spun, heading for Torment from the right side, while Spike charged from the left, his stubby legs working furiously. They arrived almost simultaneously. Torment ignored Spike, and the little dinosaur slammed into him at full tilt, all four horns driving deep into the black wolf's side. A moment later, the salamander reached down and touched Torment's shoulder, and leaping flames ran across his back. His ice-blue eyes, still on Alice, were framed in crimson and orange fire.

His lips parted, slowly, and he gave his wet, nasty chuckle.

"Is that," he said, "the best you can do?"

Torment's forepaw swept around, taking the salamander's legs out from underneath it. More flame blazed along the labyrinthine's fur where he touched the fire-creature, but he seemed unconcerned. He opened his jaws wide, wider than any wolf had a right to, until he looked like a snake about to swallow an egg. With a mighty *snap*, they closed on the oval twist of flame the salamander had in place of a head. All the fires went out at once, like a snuffed candle, and wisps of acrid black smoke rose from Torment's scorched fur.

Spike was struggling to get his balance back after embedding his horns in the labyrinthine's hide. Before he could free himself, Torment gave a wild shake, like a dog climbing out of a pond, and the dinosaur was suddenly flying through the air to crash upside down into one of the statues. The black wolf was on him in a moment, pouncing almost playfully, and he struck at Spike's exposed belly. The dinosaur was armored all over with thick plating, but Torment's claw went through it as if it were butter. Alice doubled over in pain as her creature died, feeling as if someone had driven a knife into her stomach. Through blinding tears, she could see Isaac staggering against a statue, similarly affected.

"Sister Alice! Brother Isaac!" Dex spun, turning her back on the wolves, and charged Torment. Alice wanted to cry out, but her lungs had seized up, and for the moment she could only whimper. Torment gave Dex a pitying look, but a moment later his eyes crossed in pain as she buried one of her swords in his nose. The huge wolf gave an irritated grunt and actually retreated a step, but not before the other silver blade opened a cut on his forepaw, leaking thick, black blood.

Torment growled, a low rumbling sound like a truck engine. He snapped at Dex, who dodged lithely aside, leaving another cut on the wolf's cheek. But Torment kept coming, ignoring his wounds, and Dex was forced to give ground.

Alice found enough air to shout a warning. "Dex! Behind you!"

It came a moment too late. A shaggy brown wolf, creeping out from behind a statue, had positioned itself square in Dex's path. As she backed toward it, it lunged, jaws closing on her ankle. The caryatid's armor kept its teeth from her skin, but it still managed to pull her leg out from under her, leaving her unbalanced. As she fought to steady herself, Torment swiped at her with a paw, sending her flying backward. She landed on the ground with a *crunch* and a clatter of armor, silver swords skittering across the stone.

Torment's tongue came out again, licking the cut on his nose. His eyes narrowed, and he padded toward Dex's fallen form.

I have to stop him. Alice struggled to her feet, breathing hard. *I have to . . .*

Run. The Dragon's voice echoed through her skull.

No! These are my—my friends. I'm not going to leave them!

You misunderstand. Get Torment's attention, and then run. He will follow.

Alice blinked. *What if he doesn't?*

He will. He is my brother, but he is still part wolf, and it is in his nature to chase the prey that flees.

Right. Alice cast about for a moment, not sure *how* to

get the labyrinthine's attention. She spotted Soranna, who had been hiding among the statues but was now creeping out toward Torment. All she had was her spear, but she obviously meant to try to attack the giant wolf, suicidal as that might seem. *She's braver than she gives herself credit for.*

"Soranna!" Alice hissed. The girl looked around, and Alice held up her hand. "Throw me the spear!"

Soranna complied, and Alice snatched the spear of moon-stuff out of the air. It was almost weightless, with a point like a needle. Alice wrapped herself in Spike's supernatural strength, lifted the weapon, and sent it flying into Torment's flank. It flashed through the air, a shaft of solid moonlight, and buried itself a foot deep in the labyrinthine's ebony fur.

Torment staggered under the blow, and his head snapped around. Alice waited a moment until she was certain she had his full attention. Then she looked him in the eye, stuck out her tongue, and ran for it.

She sprinted down a narrow alley between the statues, ducking under the stone warriors' outstretched arms and unsheathed weapons. Wolves tried to come at her from the sides, but Alice outpaced them, dodging snapping jaws. One beast emerged in her path, and Alice lowered her shoulder and slammed into it with her best footballer's tackle. With Spike's strength behind her, the wolf went flying.

Risking a look over her shoulder, she saw Torment in pursuit, shouldering the statues aside or snapping them to pieces in his jaws. Alice wrapped the Swarm thread around herself, to protect her skin from flying splinters, and ducked out past the last rank of statues and through the doorway.

The corridor outside was deserted, but not for long. Three wolves were hard on her heels, and she could hear more furry feet padding after her. *That's good. The more that follow me, the fewer the others have to deal with.* As long as Torment himself kept coming, Isaac could probably handle any wolves that were left behind. *And Dex, if she's . . . if she's okay.* Alice desperately hoped the caryatid's armor had provided enough protection to blunt Torment's claws.

Doorways came up on both sides. Alice took the first turn, hearing the claws of the wolves scrabbling on the slick stone, and pounded down another corridor. She was just looking over her shoulder when she caught a flash of movement from a doorway to one side.

It was a wolf, in mid-leap. Alice tried to sidestep, but she was moving too quickly, and the beast fastened its jaws on her arm. Its teeth ripped a great ragged hole in her sleeve, but her Swarm-hardened skin proved too tough for them. Even so, the momentum of the creature pulled her to the ground, and girl and wolf went down together in a rolling heap of fur and flailing limbs.

Alice ended up on the bottom, on her back. The wolf released her arm and went for her face, jaws wide. Alice could smell its hot, stinking breath, like rancid meat. She jammed her hand under its muzzle, pushing it up and away, and gathered her legs underneath her. She planted both her bare feet in its belly, fur soft between her toes, and shoved with all of Spike's strength. The wolf was launched into the air so hard it rebounded off the ceiling and landed in a whimpering heap.

Alice scrambled to her feet and ran. The next turn led to a corridor with a half-dozen wolves blocking the way, and Alice headed back the way she'd come. She ran down another corridor, and reached the next doorway just in time to see a pair of wolves saunter into the hallway behind her. They weren't running anymore, just padding after her, jaws open and tongues lolling, as though mocking her earlier gesture of defiance.

They're playing with me. The realization woke a deep, smoldering rage. Torment *is playing with me. He's got me going around in circles.* She'd forgotten, in her haste to get away, that the labyrinth included the interior of the keep. *He wants me to keep running until I drop.* The Dragon had been right about its brother's animal nature.

Okay. Alice tried to calm her mind. *I've got his attention. I need to keep it. Now what?*

He's not the only one who can play tricks with the labyrinth . . .

"I'm really sorry about this," Alice muttered out of the corner of her mouth.

The swarmer dipped its beak, regarding her with beady black eyes, almost as if it understood. Alice hefted it carefully, testing its weight, then leaned around the corner. There were three wolves waiting there with their backs to her. They'd expected her to come from the other direction, but a little twist to the labyrinth had put her behind them instead.

She stepped out, quiet in her bare feet, and hefted the swarmer. *I wish I'd paid a little bit more attention when the boys played baseball in the street.*

Any deficiencies in her technique, however, were

more than compensated for by the prodigious strength of her throwing arm and the active assistance of the "ball." She hurled the swarmer overarm in a fast arc, its beak aimed squarely at the wolves. The little creature twisted in midair to stay in position, and it slammed into the hindquarters of one beast hard enough to drive its beak several inches into the thing's rump. The wolf yipped in pain, squirming frantically to get its jaws on the swarmer. Alice let the little thing vanish and ducked back around the corner as the other two wolves spun and came after her.

As they rounded the doorway with a screech of claws on stone, they were met by the massed ranks of the Swarm, lined up like tiny soldiers. Taloned feet made a *tiktiktiktik* sound on the stone as the little creatures charged, beaks slashing and stabbing. The wolves fought back for a moment, and one of them even got a swarmer in its mouth, but its teeth were unable to make an impression on the rubbery little thing. The wolf yelped as the swarmer poked its tongue, and scrambled after its companion, who was already beating a hasty retreat.

Alice sent the Swarm in pursuit, keeping a few steps behind. The two fleeing wolves stampeded the third one, who had been turning in circles searching for the vanished swarmer, and the three of them set off down the corridor chased by a tide of little black bodies. Alice, her mind half on the labyrinth-fabric, felt Torment react furiously. More wolves burst out of side corridors ahead of them, and others appeared from doorways behind her. Reunited with the rest of their pack, the three fleeing animals turned to attack. The swarmers bounced every which way, kicked and hurled from the wolves' jaws, as though a bunch of overexcited dogs had been set loose on a room full of tennis balls.

Alice let the Swarm disappear. There was a doorway just ahead of her, and she reached out for the fabric, twisting a path between here and there that took her back onto familiar territory. She plunged through to find herself in the garden room, with its bushes, its flowing fountain, and its enormous central—

—*tree.* Alice grinned. She let go of Spike's thread, which snapped back in quivering relief, and pulled the tree-sprite's around and around herself, until she began to change.

Through the green-on-green eyes of the sprite, the dead stone all around her was vague, gray and lacking in details. But when she looked at the bushes, she saw them with stark clarity. They stood out in beautiful colors, not just the leaves, but a hundred subtle movements under the surface—she could even see water moving upward through the branches by capillary action, nutrients slowly leached from the soil to be shuttled to growing buds, and all the other processes that drove the life of a plant. The wolves, behind her, were a mass of dull red animal shapes, ugly and incomprehensible.

But the tree, ahead of her, was the most startling thing of all. It was *alive* in a way Alice had never really grasped, less a single organism than a whole colony budded from a single seed, stretching from the thinnest root tendrils in the soil to the leaves that hung from the branches. Scrambling forward to put her green-skinned hand against it, Alice could feel the slow, gentle pulse of its life energy. She felt the strain it was under, growing in these unnatural conditions—surrounded by stone, kept watered and fed only by magic.

And she felt it twist and shudder, eager to reshape itself in response to her commands. A branch curled down toward her, as easily as if it were her own arm, and she grabbed it with both hands and let it lift her up into the canopy. The wolves were pouring into the room, surrounding the planter and blocking the doorway. The bolder members of the pack sniffed the air near the tree and stared up at Alice's diminutive green form.

There's only one way out of here, Alice thought. Her lip curved upward. *They think they've got me cornered.* All the better. *While they're here, they're leaving the others alone.*

Bark rippled out from where she touched the tree, flowing across her body like water, then hardening into a dense, raspy armor. Her fingers became claws like splintered branches. Where her feet rested on the branch, the armor merged with the bark of the tree itself, as though Alice were a branch herself.

The first wolf scratched at the bark with its claws. Alice bent the tree's biggest limb back until it was taut as a bow, then let it loose. It snapped down with the force of a sledgehammer, leaves scraping and rustling against the ground, catching the wolf in its midsection and flinging the beast into the wall. Another limb whipped into the next-nearest wolf, bowling it over into several of its fellows.

The wolves attacked en masse, in a wave of frothing muzzles and slashing claws. They ran at the tree, biting at the branches as they swished by, and threw themselves at the trunk, trying to pull themselves up by their claws to get at Alice's high perch. All the tree's limbs went into action, like a great leafy octopus, slamming the creatures back or wrapping around them and flinging them aside. Their claws and teeth did no more than slash the bark of her mighty wooden partner, while its awesome strength wreaked havoc.

Soon the wounded were creeping out of the melee, backing away, hopping down from the planter and out of range of the branches, but Alice didn't intend to let them go so easily. The soil at the base of the tree *foamed* and sprouted hundreds of tiny white tendrils, snaking outward like eyeless worms. The wolves snapped at them, severing a few only to find dozens of others wrapping around their legs and paws. When a strand got a hold, it started to thicken into a more substantial root, growing faster than the desperate animal could chew through it.

It seemed like only moments had passed, but the battle was over. A few wolves retreated through the open doorway, but the rest were helpless; hurled about by the branches and now webbed over by a thick matting of tree roots that covered every inch of the stone floor like a living carpet. Alice, riding a branch, did a full circle of the tree and smiled in satisfaction.

A shadow blocked the doorway, obscuring the lanterns in the corridor outside.

"I am getting *awfully* sick of you," Torment said.

He pushed into the room, carefully, only just able to fit through the doorway. The roots he trod on crunched and splintered under his weight.

"I am beginning to think," he went on, "that my *dear* sister has played me false. Perhaps she sent you here to make certain everything went wrong? Or perhaps she simply underestimated you." He took another long step forward. "Either way, I am going to *very* much enjoy tearing out your throat."

The roots sprang at him, hundreds of tendrils wrapping around all four of his paws. They thickened as quickly as she could make them grow, into tough, finger-sized vines. Torment looked down, then back up at Alice.

"And what do you expect *this* to accomplish? You think you're going to stop me with a *plant*?" Torment raised his forepaw. There was a moment of strain as the roots struggled to hold him in place, but the black wolf's strength was immense. With a chorus of *cracks* and *pops*, the restraining tendrils snapped and shredded.

"I am a *labyrinthine*," Torment said as he ripped another paw free. "Do you have any idea what that means, girl? We are the true masters of this world, the lords of creation, and if not for you *humans* and your *books*—"

He tore himself free entirely and sprang forward, covering the distance to the tree in a single leap. Branches slammed into him from all sides, stiffened leaves with razor-sharp edges cut into him, but Torment ignored the buffeting and the blades. He turned his head sideways, opening his maw wider and wider, until he could fit the entire trunk of the tree between his teeth. Then, with unbelievable strength, he forced his jaws closed. Wood popped, groaned, and splintered, and the tree branches whipped desperately at the black wolf's muzzle. He twisted his head, and the whole top of the tree came away, leaves rustling madly. With a contemptuous twist of his jaws, he hurled it aside.

Alice was shaken free, landing amid the carpet of roots. Torment padded to the edge of the planter, looking down at her with ice-blue eyes.

"Have you had enough?" he said wearily. "Ready to lay down and die?"

Alice thought of the others, back in the throne room. Hopefully they would have gotten out of there by now. Every minute she kept Torment's attention here, with her, was a minute where he couldn't set them to running in circles. It wasn't much of a chance, but it was all she could do.

Never give up. Not ever.

The tree-sprite's lips were not really designed for human speech, but Alice managed to make them form words.

"Not ever," she said.

Torment growled, and leaped for her throat.

CHAPTER TWENTY-FIVE
END OF THE LINE

ALICE WORKED THE THREADS faster than she ever had before, letting the tree-sprite fall away and pulling on the Swarm. It was so quick, she passed from one creature's form to the other without ever becoming human in between. Her bark armor bulged, then split like a kernel of popcorn, releasing a horde of tiny black swarmers. The little creatures scuttled madly through the fallen branches of the wrecked tree, hopping over twigs and ducking through small spaces. Torment landed on the remains of the tree-sprite, shattering it to fragments under his massive paws. His jaws snapped at a swarmer near the back of the pack, but not quickly enough to catch it.

It took Torment a moment to smash the branches out of the way, and in that moment the Swarm flowed back together near the doorway, recombining into Alice's familiar body. This time she didn't bother to taunt the labyrinthine, just turned and ran. Out the door and into the corridor, ready to lose herself in the maze of hallways—

She felt the fabric of the labyrinth *jerk* under her feet. She stumbled, passing through the doorway. The corridor she'd been expecting was gone, and in its place she'd stepped into a large, square room that looked like some kind of storehouse. There was *stuff* piled against the walls: a giant mirror in a gilded frame, a pile of winter coats, an armchair lying on its side, trunks and strongboxes piled high or lying open and empty on the floor, even a suit of medieval armor on a wooden stand that looked like it belonged in some European castle. Everything was covered in dust, as though the room had not been used in a long time.

Alice just had time to glance around before Torment came through the doorway behind her, a huge cloud of dust billowing around his feet as he skidded to a stop. He was panting, dark red tongue lolling over his teeth. Slaver and thick, black blood dripped from his jaws.

"*Enough,*" he growled, so loud that the piles of junk shivered and rattled at the word. "No more doorways. No more hide-and-seek. No more games."

He stalked forward. Alice slid off to the side, hoping to find room to make a dash past him to continue her flight, but her chest went tight when she looked at the opposite wall. The doorway was gone. She was trapped in a room with no exits, alone with the great black wolf. She reached for the labyrinth-fabric, but Torment's grip was all around her, pressing down hard, and she didn't have the strength to fight it.

"This is *my* place," Torment said. "My sanctum. My private stash." He looked around, through the billows of dust. "I suppose I should clean up more often. But it has the advantage that, whatever happens, we will *not be interrupted.*" His tongue flicked across his teeth. "I want to savor this."

Alice backed up, looking desperately around in the junk. *There has to be something here, something I can use—* But she didn't think Torment would be foolish enough to bring her somewhere with any kind of a weapon. *Think, think, think—*

The huge wolf pounced, and all other thoughts were forced from her mind. Alice threw herself to one side, dodging the snap of his jaws but ending up on her back in the dust. Before she could get to her feet, he stepped on her chest, pinning her to the ground. He put only a fraction of his weight on it, but the pressure was still enough to make her cry out in pain.

Torment's muzzle slid into view, topped by his cold, blue eyes.

"You led me on quite a chase, girl," the labyrinthine said. "If that offers you any comfort."

Think, think, think. *Never give up. Not ever.* But there was nothing left. Torment had already demonstrated how easily he could deal with Spike, and there was no tree here to batter him with. She could split into the Swarm and try to hide amidst the detritus, but that would only delay the inevitable, and he could get his jaws on some of the swarmers before she could get them to cover. She had the devilfish, but neither a greenish glow nor a transformation into a gasping, flopping sea creature seemed like they would provide any advantages. *That only leaves—*

Her mental grip tightened on the black thread. The one she'd never been able to move. The Dragon.

As usual, it didn't respond when she tugged on it. This time, she bore down, tightening her mental grip, and pulled harder. Then harder still, as hard as she had ever exerted herself in the strange world of magic, and then harder still.

If she'd been pulling with her hands, they would have been scraped raw, or sliced to the bone by the taut, humming thread. But she was pulling with her *self*, all her energy and spirit, and the feeling was much worse than that. She felt as though the thread had gone into her chest and tied itself around her breastbone, with a boulder at the other end. Every tug produced sparks of pain, shooting from her fingers to her toes, like electric shocks running over her body. It felt as though she was on the verge of tearing herself to pieces, turning herself inside out, that whatever was doing the pulling would tear free from the fragile prison of her flesh like a rotten tooth ripped out of its socket.

Stop. The Dragon's voice echoed down the thread. *You must stop.*

I can't.

You will die.

If this doesn't work, I'll die anyway.

You don't understand.

I don't have time to understand. Distantly, in the real world, she could feel Torment's breath on her face. Her body was falling away, a numb and distant shadow. *This is all I have left.*

I— There was a hint of something in the Dragon's voice, an emotion she'd never heard before. *Alice—*

I won't give up. Alice gathered her strength for one last pull. *I won't.*

She felt something give way. All the air rushed out of her lungs in a gasp, and darkness crashed down on her.

She never lost consciousness, exactly. It was as though she really had torn herself away from her body, and now she floated alone in an endless black void.

Am I dead? She didn't know. She wasn't sure what it felt like to be dead.

Then she heard something. Just a distant buzz at first, like a fly tapping at a window, but it strengthened and resolved into words.

"—you." Torment's voice.

"Me." The Dragon. But not echoing around her own skull. It was real sound, out in the real world.

"That's not possible," Torment said. "You can't be *here*."

"Nevertheless," said the Dragon.

"You swore you would not oppose us."

"I know," said the Dragon. It sounded resigned. "Nevertheless."

"You're helping *her*?" Torment seemed nearly hysterical. "You have kept your oath for *two thousand years*, and now you throw it away for this *girl*?"

"Yes," the Dragon rumbled. "You would not understand."

"But she is our sister's plaything! Have you changed your convictions after so many centuries in limbo?"

"I have changed nothing."

"Then you ought to kill her and be done with it," Torment snarled. "What good can she be to *you*?"

"As I said," the Dragon repeated, "you would not understand."

Feeling was starting to return to Alice, making her aware that she still had a body after all. Every muscle ached, and her breath came in short gasps. Her heart was beating so hard she thought it might explode. But the bright, silver pain, the feeling of the thread tearing her to pieces, was gone.

She opened her eyes. Vague blurs in front of her started to resolve.

"Alice," the Dragon said. "Can you hear me?"

Alice found that she was still lying on her back, but the weight of Torment's paw was gone. She forced herself to breathe deep, tasting the ancient dust.

"I can hear you," she said. It came out as a croak. "What happened?"

"You called for me," the Dragon said. "And I came."

Alice sat up. The movement made the world whirl around her for a few moments, and she thought she might pass out. She focused on deep breaths, eyes closed, and bit by bit she settled down. When she opened her eyes again, she could see clearly, and she had to stifle a gasp.

As big as Torment was, he was tiny beside the Dragon. The huge six-legged creature nearly filled the room, curled protectively around Alice in a wall of flat white scales the size of dinner plates. Torment was sprawled in front of her, on his back as Alice had been, with one of the Dragon's feet on his stomach and its claw pressed against his throat. The Dragon's diamond-shaped head, itself almost bigger than Torment, hovered menacingly over the black wolf. A row of three hemispherical, insectoid eyes regarded Alice, and the tip of the Dragon's tail twitched gently on the flagstones beside her.

"You told me to stop," Alice said. "I thought . . ."

"We will speak of it later," the Dragon said. "First, I believe you wanted to ask my brother a question."

Alice climbed shakily to her feet. Her legs wobbled, threatening to give way beneath her, and she staggered sideways into something firm and warm that bore her weight. She looked down to find herself propped on the end of the Dragon's tail.

"I understand," Torment said. "Now I understand. He's been helping you all along. I don't know *why*, or how you've bound him, but it's no wonder Ending thinks you'll be useful—"

"Enough," the Dragon said. "Alice. Ask."

Alice stepped forward, satisfied herself that she could remain upright this time, and walked over to Torment. The black wolf looked up at her, blue eyes full of hatred and frustration.

"What happened to my father?"

"What?" Torment gave a pained chuckle. "How should I know—"

"You cannot lie," the Dragon rumbled. "Not to *me*. I have known you too long."

"Esau sent Vespidian to my house to make my father some kind of an offer," Alice said. "What did he want?"

"He wanted *you*, of course," Torment said.

"Why?" Alice asked.

"One of Esau's agents caught the scent of you. A powerful talent, bound to no master. But someone was protecting you, so he sent that idiot sprite to try to make a deal with your father."

Alice nodded slowly. That jibed with what she already knew—that Geryon had shielded her and her father from the eyes of other Readers since she'd been born. *But—*

"And then what? My father left me behind. He took a ship to South America, and it disappeared. What happened?"

"How should I know?"

The Dragon rumbled, a deep, menacing sound, and pressed its claw fractionally deeper into the black wolf's throat.

"You spied on Esau, of course," it said. "All of you spy on your masters. You saw what happened that night. You will show her." The Dragon's tail curved around to point at the giant mirror in its gaudy frame. "This is a seeing-glass, is it not?"

"A what?" Alice said, looking at it curiously.

"A device for looking at distant places, through the

eyes of invisible spirits. It can recall anything its spirits have seen for its master." The Dragon cocked its head at Torment. "And you said this was *your* place."

"All right. All right!" Torment laughed, a nasty damp sound, like a retching cough. "But you may not like what you see."

"*Show me,*" Alice said.

Torment's paw waved, feebly. The surface of the mirror went black except for tiny speckles of light that sparkled like diamond dust. The stars, Alice realized. Patches of deeper darkness resolved into clouds, drifting slowly across the sky. Toward the bottom of the mirror, the darkness was absolute, until a small patch of bright, steady lights drifted into view.

It was a ship, under way at night in a calm sea, cheery navigation lights ablaze. They were too far away to read the name painted on the bow, but Alice could make a pretty good guess.

CHAPTER TWENTY-SIX
THE *GIDEON*, REPRISE

ONCE SHE GOT THE hang of the mirror's perspective, Alice realized that the point of view—presumably Esau's—was flying through the air, well above the *Gideon* and moving at a terrific speed. Now and then other creatures came into view alongside for a few moments before dropping back. Alice recognized some of them, the flying fish-like things the apprentices had battled at the broken bridge, and some of the huge bat-moths. There were others as well, strange monsters glimpsed too briefly to get an idea of their form, momentary flashes of brilliantly colored wings, taloned limbs, or writhing, squid-like tentacles. The mirror's view remained locked frustratingly forward, where the ship was growing larger.

The *Gideon* was a handsome single-funnel steamer, smartly painted in gray, blue, and red, with cheerful yellow stripes on the hull. Electric lights burned on its rails and from the top of the funnel, rocking only slightly in the calm sea. As Esau approached, more lights came on, all along the boxy superstructure. The crew had sighted the approaching Reader and his accompanying minions, but they had no idea what to do—the ship's wake kicked up higher as it increased speed, and the white-jacketed crewmen on deck lined the rail, staring in disbelief at the monsters approaching from the sky.

They were soon joined by the passengers, alerted by the shouting that something was amiss. A couple of dozen men and women in their sleepwear stumbled up from belowdecks, and started shouting—Alice was surprised to find she could hear them through the mirror—demanding to know what was going on. Then a young woman caught sight of what was coming, and her scream cut through the babble. Everyone looked up and was immediately transfixed, eyes wide in wonder or terror. One woman fainted dead away into the arms of the man beside her, and a little girl, younger than Alice, began to cry.

Only one man didn't seem surprised. A lump formed

in Alice's throat as she recognized her father, pushing his way through the crowd to the rail. Even in his night-shirt, he looked calmer and more in control than the uniformed crewmen. The wind of the ship's passage tugged at his hair, and his sleeves flapped wildly.

Esau descended until he was level with the rail, hovering over the ocean a few yards from the ship. Above him, his escorting creatures spread out, flapping over the deck of the ship, mostly invisible except as silhouettes against the stars or the funnel lights.

"Hello, Mr. Creighton," he said. His voice sounded cracked and ancient, but at the same time shot through with power. It was the voice of an Old Testament prophet laying down the Law. "You should have considered my offer."

"Damn your offer," Alice's father said. "It doesn't matter how many monsters you bring with you, the answer's still the same."

"Fortunately," Esau said, "your cooperation is no longer required. I will simply take this ship apart until I find what I'm looking for."

"No!" Alice's father hesitated. None of the other people on deck seemed to understand the Reader's words, but they saw the conversation, and a wide, empty circle had formed around him. Some of the passengers were fleeing back belowdecks, or to the other side of the ship. More children were wailing in terror.

"These people have nothing to do with this," Alice's father said. "Listen! Alice—she's not here! I swear it!"

"I find that unlikely," Esau said. "After protecting her so carefully, I doubt you would simply leave her behind. But in either case, best to make certain."

"She is *not here!*" Alice's father looked around wildly. "Take me, if that's what you've come to do. Kill me if you have to. No one else here deserves to suffer!"

"I'm afraid it's a little late for that, Mr. Creighton," Esau said. "You might have given that a thought before you got on board."

At a gesture from the Reader, huge black tentacles shot out of the water, rising straight up like rubbery pillars. They curled downward, fastening around the ship, crushing the railing with a shriek of twisting metal. The decks groaned and popped, and glass shattered in the windows. Alice heard the *crack* of gunshots, as some brave crewman fired a pistol into the thing, with as little effect as a slingshot on an elephant.

"Damn you," Alice's father said. "*Damn* you!"

"Now, now, Mr. Creighton," Esau said. "I tried to do this politely."

There was another *crack*, louder than the pistol, and a simultaneous explosion of light. One of the moth-bats was outlined for an instant in the brilliant white glow of a lightning bolt. It burst into flame, folding up and falling into the sea.

The point of view shifted as Esau looked up. The sky, which had been clear moments before, was now a mass of dark thunderheads, illuminated from within by a continuous, flickering barrage of lightning. At the forefront of the storm hung a single dark figure, outlined by the wild bolts of electricity.

"I ought to have known!" Esau shouted, above the roar of the wind.

He rose, hovering above the ship. The dark figure came closer.

"You can never keep your nose out of my business!" Esau said.

"The opportunity was too good to miss," the dark figure said. "It's not often I can lure you out of hiding."

"And I, in turn, appreciate the opportunity to destroy you once and for all."

A bolt of lightning slashed between them. In that brief

303

moment, as bright light illuminated the shadowed figure, its face was burned into Alice's retina. It was a face she knew well.

Geryon.

Esau gestured sharply, and the flock of creatures around him soared upward toward the other Reader. More lightning flashed out to intercept them. Behind the cage of brilliant white bolts, Geryon raised his hands, and the storm cloud beside him formed itself into an enormous fanged maw, with crackling slivers of liquid electricity for teeth. It opened wide, as though taking a deep breath, and then exhaled a plume of silver-white flame that reached out toward Esau.

Esau fought back. More creatures popped into being, stranger and stranger things, winging or crawling or stalking their way through the air toward Geryon. Bolts of lightning answered them, blasts of fire, gusts of wind as sharp as razors, beams of utter darkness that disintegrated everything they touched.

It was like a battle between gods from an ancient legend, magic on a scale beyond Alice's comprehension.

But her eyes were drawn to something else.

Down below, ignored by both combatants, the *Gideon* was burning.

"My master was forced to withdraw," Torment said. "A temporary setback, he called it. Afterward, Geryon claimed you. To the victors go the spoils, I suppose." The labyrinthine gave another wet chuckle. "Esau was angry. He sent Vespidian to try to—"

"I know that part," Alice snapped.

She understood, suddenly, why so many people—Ending, Ashes, Mr. Black, even Torment himself—were so bitter toward the Readers. *They're like . . . like children, scuffling on top of an anthill. They don't care who gets crushed underfoot. They don't even think about it!*

He is a Reader, Ending had told her. *His magic is based on cruelty and death.*

"Enough." The Dragon's voice, almost gentle, in spite of its depth and power. "Good-bye, brother."

"Wait!" Alice shouted as Torment squirmed helplessly under the Dragon's claw. "You can't—"

There was a *crunch* of breaking bone, and the point of the Dragon's talon drove itself through the wolf's throat, releasing a gush of thick black blood. After a moment, Torment began to evaporate, blood and all, into a pall of noxious smoke. Within a few seconds, he was gone.

Long seconds passed as Alice strove to master herself. Finally, she said, "You killed him? Your own brother?"

"No," the Dragon said. "It takes more than that to destroy a labyrinthine for good. But let us say . . . we will not see him for some time."

"Oh."

Alice walked to the mirror. Its surface had gone silver again, and she put out one hand, feeling the cool glass under her fingers. She stood there for a long time, eyes closed.

CHAPTER TWENTY-SEVEN
REUNION

AFTER A WHILE, SHE felt the warm, dry weight of the tip of the Dragon's tail curling around her shoulders.

"Alice," the Dragon said. "I am sorry."

"Thank you for helping me," Alice said. "I thought . . ." She shook her head and wrapped her arms tight across her chest. "I thought I was going to die."

"You might have," the Dragon said. "You have a great deal of talent, but as a Reader you are still just beginning. When a Reader summons a creature, it is her energy that sustains it, calls it into this world from the world of the prison-book. The more powerful the creature, the more energy is required. Your energy was not sufficient to summon me, and the attempt to do so was tearing you apart."

Alice's voice was a whisper. "So what happened?"

"I used my own power to . . . make up the difference, you might say. It cost me a great deal. Replenishing my power is difficult while I am imprisoned."

"Oh." Alice blinked away her tears. "I'm sorry."

"No. You had no alternative, and Torment needed to be . . . dealt with. However, it does mean I will not be able to appear in this way for some time. Perhaps quite a long time. Even speaking to you will be difficult. I will . . . sleep, if you like."

"I don't . . . I didn't want that." Alice took hold of the Dragon's tail and pressed it to her cheek. She felt a sudden closeness to this vast, alien creature, with its insect-black eyes. It was the way it spoke to her—without sentimentality or condescension, like an equal. She felt tears pricking her eyes again. "But I need your help. I still have to find my father."

"Alice . . ." the Dragon said.

"Could Torment have been . . . lying, in the magic mirror?"

"No. Not here. Not to me."

"Then the ship really did go down." Alice balled her hands into fists. "It has to be something else, then.

One of them sucked him into a book, or some creature grabbed him, or . . ."

She trailed off. *That can't be* it. *Not just like that.* The world could not bring her all this way, through all these dangers, for this to be the end. In a place full of magic— of swarmers and Readers and talking cats—there had to be a way out. *There* has *to be.*

"Alice." The Dragon's voice was soft. "What motive would Esau or Geryon have to do such a thing?"

"I don't *know!*" Alice said. "Geryon lied to me. He's been lying to me all along. Who knows what his real plans are?"

The Dragon's head swung around in front of her. She could see herself reflected in its trio of dark eyes, three tiny, haggard girls staring back at her.

"There has to be *something*," Alice said in a small voice. "Or else . . . what was the point of any of this? What's the point of *anything*?" She sucked in a long breath, fighting tears. "What am I supposed to do now?"

The Dragon was quiet for a long time. Alice could hear the puff of its breath, like a vast bellows.

"There is a great deal I could tell you," it said, finally. "But if I did, I would be no better than the others, who think to use you as a tool for their own ends. Do you remember when you came to fight me, in the prison-book?"

Alice laughed hollowly. "I'm not likely to forget."

"Do you know why I submitted to you, rather than fighting to the end?"

She shook her head.

"I thought you were there at my sister's direction. It is her way to use everyone around her as a part of her plans, whether they are aware of it or not. In this, she is no better than Geryon. But you . . . I felt that you would not be used. Would not *allow* yourself to be used. You deserve the opportunity to make your own choices, to walk your own path. Indeed, I believe you will do so, regardless of what Ending, Geryon, or anyone else intends. You must do what you believe to be right."

"Right?" Alice said. "What if I can't tell for certain?"

The Dragon's face was immobile, but Alice thought she heard a smile in its voice. "Which of us can?"

It was too much to think about, and Alice was too tired. She felt drained, cored, like a rind of fruit after it had been squeezed for juice.

"Right now," she said, "all I want to do is go home." That meant the Library, she realized. Her small room on

310

the third floor, with the cracks in the ceiling, the book lying half read on her pillow, and the two threadbare rabbits standing silent sentry by the window. She shook her head, fighting the exhaustion. "But the others. I need to get back to them."

"Yes. This is good-bye, then. For a time. Someday you will be a powerful enough Reader in your own right to call me up and bend me to your will." The Dragon inclined its head. "I hope, when that day comes, you remember . . . moments like this, when you were in the power of another. It is something that the other Readers, I fear, have forgotten."

"I will." Alice climbed to her feet, shrugging the Dragon's tail off of her shoulders. "Thank you."

The Dragon's black tongue flicked out between its teeth, tasting the air. "Good luck."

Then, with a rush of air that set the dust to swirling, the vast creature was gone.

Alice was glad to find that the Dragon's disappearance did not remove her ability to manipulate the labyrinth. But Torment's absence was like a vast wound in the fabric, and without his power to maintain the twisted, folded space, it was unraveling. For the moment, it was still solid enough that Alice, eyes closed, could pull a doorway into the storeroom, and then connect it to the throne room.

Before going through, she looked around at the accumulated junk piled against the walls. Some of it was probably valuable, or magical, or both, but she couldn't bring herself to paw through the hoard. She turned her back on it and stepped through, letting the path close behind her, arriving in the throne room mid-argument.

"—you're hardly in good enough shape for that," Isaac was saying. "And even if they have gone, it doesn't mean that Torment has."

"We cannot simply sit here and do nothing." It was Dex's voice, and Alice's heart leaped. "Sister Alice is in danger, and we must go to her assistance."

"She's right," Soranna agreed quietly. "She would come for us."

"I know," Isaac said. "I'll go, but the two of you should stay here—"

"Um," Alice said. "Hi."

Isaac spun, coat flaring around him. "Alice?"

"Yeah," Alice said. "I—"

She was caught unprepared as he ran right at her, wrapping his arms around her in a fierce hug. For a moment Alice stood ramrod-straight, not sure what to do. Then she softened, and brought her hands up tentatively to grip his shoulders.

"I thought . . ." Isaac's voice was a whisper in her ear. "I thought you had died on me, too."

"I'm okay." It was all Alice could think to say. "Really. I'm okay."

He stepped aside, wiping his eyes with his sleeve. But hugs were apparently the order of the day, and Dex was next in line. One half of her face was purpling into a monstrous bruise, and she walked with a limp, but otherwise her encounter with Torment seemed to have left her none the worse for wear. She put her arms around Alice, and Alice hugged her back, gently, not sure where Dex was hurt.

"I was worried about you," Alice said. "After Torment cut through Spike so easily, when he hit you . . ."

"The caryatid protected me most excellently," Dex said, pulling away. "I was just telling Brother Isaac that this expedition has been more successful than most in that respect." She raised her arm, with the circular scar where it had been severed and reattached. "After all, I am still in one piece!"

Alice couldn't help but smile.

Dex stepped back, revealing Soranna, standing awkwardly with her hands behind her back. She looked at Alice, uncertain, and Alice stepped forward to hug her as well.

"But what happened?" Isaac said, over Soranna's shoulder. "Where's Torment?"

"Gone," Alice said. "Banished."

"You—" He shook his head. "How did you do that?"

"It's a long story," Alice said. "And for now I think we'd better get out of here, or else we're going to have a very long walk."

She reached out for the unraveling fabric of the labyrinth and folded a long path, from the throne room to the portal-book. Cold air from the outside gusted in through the doorway. Then she glanced back at the dais, where Jacob had fallen. There was something there now, a glittering pyramid of ice.

Isaac followed her gaze. "I sealed him in," he said. "It should last for a while. When our masters clean this place out, I'll make sure they bring him back to me. He deserves that."

Alice swallowed and nodded. She led the way, out the door and across the fortress by a trick of folded space, back to where they'd begun.

CHAPTER TWENTY-EIGHT
HOMECOMING

FOR A MOMENT THE throne room, via an eye-twisting doorway, led directly out to the long, lonely bridge on the edge of the fortress. When they were all through, Alice let go of the fabric, and they were once again on the small, circular platform where they'd first come in. On the stone pedestal sat the portal-book leading back to the cavern of front doors, right where they'd left it.

It was colder out here than it had been in the keep, and Alice hugged herself against the wind that whistled and moaned up from the abyss. The four apprentices walked over to the book and looked down at it solemnly.

"Are you going to be all right, Soranna?" Alice said. The thought had been nagging at her. "You said your master would be angry with you if you allowed yourself to be polluted with 'impure ideas.'"

Soranna gave a tiny smile. "I think I will be fine. I realize now that she has more need of me than I once believed. I am the last of my cohort, after all." She shrugged. "When she asks what happened, I will simply tell her what she wants to hear."

"Thank you, Sister Soranna," Dex said. "We would not have made it without you."

Alice hesitated. "I guess this is good-bye, then."

"It is." Soranna nodded to Isaac, and accepted a hug from Dex. "But I think I will see you again."

"I hope so," Alice said.

Soranna looked down, but her smile broadened. She turned away and flipped the book open. Between blinks, she was gone. The pages of the portal-book crackled with light for a moment, and it snapped shut with a *thump*.

"As for myself," Dex said, "I am also confident I will see you again, Sister Alice and Brother Isaac. I will consult the auguries and discover when that will be, and await the day with considerable enthusiasm."

"Thank you," Alice said. "For everything."

Dex smiled and gave a jaunty wave. She stepped up to the book, and a moment later she too was gone.

Alice looked sidelong at Isaac. His face, always thin, was now practically gaunt.

"Are you all right?" she ventured.

"No," Isaac whispered. "I'm not. Are you?"

"No. I'm . . . sorry about Evander."

"I was *right there*." Isaac's hands clenched into fists, and he thrust them into the pockets of his coat. "I was right there and I couldn't do anything."

Alice, thinking of the magic mirror in Torment's hoard, nodded in silent sympathy. "I . . ."

She hesitated, and he cocked his head. Alice took a deep breath.

"I came here," she said, "to find my father."

Isaac looked at her, uncertain, as Alice began the story. She'd never told anyone the whole thing, not like this, from the fairy in her kitchen to her ambush of Vespidian, and her desperate hope that somewhere in Esau's fortress she would find an answer. There was no one else in the world she *could* tell, no one else who knew the truth about her deal with Ending, or what had happened inside the Dragon's book. It took longer than she expected.

When she arrived at her confrontation with Torment, where she'd nearly died, Isaac's eyes went wide. Alice swallowed hard and continued, describing the scene in the magic mirror and the battle above the *Gideon*. As she reached the very end, her voice cracked.

"My father ... tried to give himself up. For all the other people on the ship. He knew what would happen. But Esau and Geryon ..."

Alice shook her head and squeezed her eyes shut. She hadn't allowed herself to cry, not since they'd told her that her father was dead; crying was what you did for someone who was really and truly gone, and she had never believed that. Tears were spilling down her cheeks now, and she was powerless to stop them.

She felt Isaac wrap his arms around her, hugging her tight, and she rested her head on his shoulder.

"What am I supposed to do now?" she whispered. "I came here to find him, to *save* him. Now ..."

Isaac pulled away, and she found herself staring into his eyes. The pain she saw there was a mirror of her own.

"I'm sorry," she said. "It's the same for you, isn't it?"

He nodded.

"I feel like I have nothing left," Alice said. "Now what?"

"I don't know," Isaac said. "But we're alive. You and I. That's something."

A long, quiet moment passed. Isaac suddenly seemed to realize how close they were to each other, noses nearly touching, and he flushed and took an awkward step back.

"What are you going to tell Geryon?" he said, after a pause.

"I don't know." Alice felt something new bubbling up inside her, a hot, bright rage that cut through the guilt and grief. "He lied to me. He's been lying to me all along. He and Esau killed my father. They didn't even mean to, it was just . . . just an *accident!*" She looked up at him, new fire in her eyes. "And your master, Anaxomander, sent your brother here to die, didn't he? He traded him like a pet. We can't let them get away with it."

"Get away with it?" Isaac looked taken aback. "They're old Readers, our *masters*. What can we possibly do?"

"I'll think of something. I'll *find* something." She looked at him speculatively. "Will you help me?"

"I . . . *if* I can." Isaac shook his head. "Be careful, Alice. I don't want you to end up like . . . like Jacob."

"I won't. I promise." Alice took a long breath and looked around the empty platform. "We should go back."

"Next time I see you," Isaac said, "it'll probably be another mission, like this one."

"Maybe."

"What if we end up on opposite sides?" Isaac shifted uncomfortably. "I don't think I could hurt you, Alice.

Whatever my master told me to do. If he sent us to fight, I'd..."

"We'd work something out." Alice forced a smile. "We always do."

Isaac gave a weak smile and nodded. He flipped the portal-book open and looked back over his shoulder.

"I'm glad you were here," he said.

Then, before she could reply, he looked down at the book and vanished. There was a flicker and a *snap* as the book slammed itself shut, and Alice was alone.

She waited a few moments, looking back at the constellation of lights that was Esau's fortress. Going back meant facing Geryon, and she wasn't sure she was ready for that. She took the black thread that led to the Dragon in her mental grip, and sighed. *I wish...*

But she was filthy, hungry, and so, so tired. She turned back to the portal-book, flipped it open, and Read herself through into the cavern. Then, summoning the devilfish for a little light, she found her way back to the boulder marked *Geryon*, and the little volume that sat on top of it. She took a deep breath, opened it, and read:

"Welcome back, Alice," Geryon said. *"We were starting to worry..."*

"Welcome back, Alice," Geryon said. "We were starting to worry that something had gone wrong."

She was standing in front of Geryon's desk, in his study, staring down at the portal-book. Geryon reached out and picked it up carefully, and put it back into its metal cube of a chest.

"How long has it been?" Alice said. Her voice felt scratchy.

"The better part of three days. I trust you successfully completed your assignment?"

Alice looked up into Geryon's smiling face. He looked almost the same as ever—the same as she'd seen in the magic mirror—but she thought she could sense a change. Something around the eyes, a tiny hint of suspicion peeking through his kindly facade. *Or is it* me *that's changed?*

"Yes, sir," she said, in a business-like tone. "Jacob is dead, and none of the other apprentices stole anything from the fortress."

"Good, good. I imagine there's a lot of cleaning up to do there."

"Yes, sir. Quite a bit."

"All in good time. You've done well, and you must be tired. We can go over the details later."

"Thank you, sir," Alice said. "I'm going to go and get some rest."

She nodded politely to Geryon, turned, and left the study. The weight of exhaustion was suddenly oppressive, and she shut the door and rested against it for a few moments.

She didn't notice Emma, as silent as a solid ghost, until she was standing right in front of her with a platter bearing a pitcher of water and a plate of sandwiches.

"For me?" Alice said.

Emma nodded.

"Please put it in my room, and then come back here," Alice said. The girl marched up the stairs at once, and Alice followed when her legs felt up to the challenge. Ascending to the third floor was a torture of aches and bruises. It felt like a thousand years ago that she'd been sprinting down the hallways of Esau's fortress with wolves in hot pursuit. Emma, platter delivered, passed her on the stairs, going back down to wait for further orders.

Ashes was curled in a tight ball outside her door. As Alice came down the corridor, he got up and wove back and forth in front of her like he was trying to get stepped on.

"She returns at last!" the cat said. "It can't have been that bad. You've still got all your limbs!"

Alice was not in the mood for Ashes' humor, and that comment only reminded her of Dex's misadventure with the crocodile. She stepped past him.

"Alice?" Ashes hurried after her. "Wait. Alice!"

For a moment she wanted to slam her door, but it wasn't really Ashes she was angry at. She left the door cracked open, and a moment later his head popped through, with the chagrined look of a cat expecting a smack.

"You are all right, aren't you?" he said. "Was it really terrible?"

"I'm fine," Alice said, though she wasn't sure that was the truth. "It was . . . hard." Then, seeing Ashes' drooping ears, she added, "Honestly, though. I'm okay. I'm just . . . very tired."

"All right," Ashes said. He still sounded dubious.

"We can talk in the morning," Alice said.

"It is the morning."

"In the evening, then. Or tomorrow. Whenever I wake up."

"Okay," Ashes said. "I'll tell Mother you're safe. She'll be glad to hear it."

I bet she will. She still didn't know what to think about Ending, or how much she was going to tell her. *Later.*

Ashes withdrew, and Alice shut the door the rest of the

way. She took the pitcher of iced water from the platter and drank quite a lot of it, then forced herself to eat one of the sandwiches. After that, her eyes started to close of their own accord, and she just managed to stagger over to the bed before sleep closed around her like a warm, fuzzy blanket.

CHAPTER TWENTY-NINE

AND IF
YOU WRONG US...

GERYON WAS RUNNING, HIS whiskers wild and disheveled, his robe flapping around him. He was in a complicated tangle of brick walls, taller than a man, marking out narrow corridors, turns, and junctions, like a maze from a children's puzzle book built full-scale. His threadbare slippers flapped and scraped against the cobblestones underfoot.

"You don't know what you're doing!" he shouted. "We'll destroy you for this! You don't have a chance!"

Alice regarded him with unblinking black eyes.

Her body was huge, six-legged, magnificently strong and armored in scales. She was the Dragon. She towered above the walls of the maze, and when she took a step forward, bricks *crunched* and exploded under her claws.

"You might as well give up!" Geryon said. He sounded as tiny and pathetic as he looked, hurrying along the brick corridors, his ample stomach bouncing with every step. "There's nothing you can do against me!"

Alice chuckled, and it was a vast, booming sound. She took another step forward, effortlessly crossing corridors it would have taken Geryon hours to get through, and put her foot down right behind the fleeing Reader. He jumped into the air at the sound of crumbling masonry, and ran even faster, zigging and zagging desperately through the maze in an effort to get away from her. It was no use, though. Every time he tried to escape, the walls of the maze turned him back, leading him inexorably on a path back toward where Alice was waiting.

"I'm warning you!" Geryon wheezed, gasping for breath. "You've got one last chance to turn back."

"You lied to me," Alice rumbled. The buzz of her voice made stones jump in the piles of rubble by her feet.

"You let my father die. You watched it happen."

"So what?" Geryon's lips turned down petulantly. "He would have died anyway. It doesn't make a bit of difference. He wasn't one of us, he didn't matter."

"Shut *up!*" Alice roared, lunging forward. She planted a huge claw on either side of him, leaning down until her shadow fell across the Reader. "You have no idea what matters. You've never *cared* about anyone but yourself. You deserve . . ."

"What?" The Reader looked fearful. "What are you going to do?"

Alice ate him. He tasted sweet, like a sticky gumdrop, and she chewed thoughtfully a few times before swallowing him down.

"Monster!" someone shouted. "You're a monster!"

She looked around, huge body coiling. The maze was gone, and in its place was a city street. Standing alone on the pavement was her father, in the nightshirt she'd seen him wearing in the magic mirror, pointing a trembling finger at her.

"No," Alice said. "Father, it's me. You don't understand."

"Kill it!" Her father bent over, picked up a stone,

and hurled it at her. It struck her in the face, and the impact *hurt*, in spite of all her size and armor. "Come on, help me!"

A small crowd was gathering. There was Miss Juniper, her tutor, and Cooper, her father's man. Mr. Pallworthy the lawyer was there, and the postman who'd always said hello to her as he went about his rounds, the librarian from the Carnegie Library, and the man who sold her favorite candy in Grand Central Station. And more, faces she couldn't put names to, everyone she'd known in the days before Geryon had come into her life and wrenched it onto a new course. Now they were all grabbing stones and throwing them at her, and she shrank under the barrage.

"Wait!" she shouted. "Father, it's *me*, it's Alice! Please!"

It was because she still had the Dragon's shape, she realized. Hurriedly, she fumbled with her threads, trying to uncoil the black one that led to the Dragon and return to human form. But her mental grip slipped off it, as though it were coated in ice, and no matter how hard she tried, the control she needed wouldn't come.

"Kill it!" her father screamed. "Kill it!"

Wailing, Alice turned and ran, pursued by a rain of stones.

She opened her eyes as the light of sunset painted her room orange. The old toys in the window threw enormous, rabbit-shaped shadows across the floor. Alice lay still for a moment, breathing hard, as the remnants of the dream chased themselves around and around inside her head.

Father . . .

Carefully, wincing at the aches in her muscles, she sat up and slid her legs out of bed.

She couldn't shake off the memory of her father's face in the dream. Twisted up, not with hate or rage, but something even worse. *Disapproval? Disappointment?*

Alice would never have thought of herself as a person who would seek revenge. It happened sometimes, in stories, usually when some old king had been done in by a villain and the heroic prince swore never to rest until the responsible party was brought to justice. Pulp heroes on the radio were always getting revenge too, for girlfriends or innocent victims of vicious criminals. It had always seemed a bit stupid to Alice. After all, met-ing out vengeance wouldn't bring the victims back, or help their loved ones forget, or do anything except pile one unfortunate tragedy on top of another.

Now, though, she understood. The cold, *helpless* feeling as she'd watched the images in the mirror play out, as Geryon and Esau fought each other and destroyed her entire life as an afterthought. And the rage, rising like bile from her stomach into the back of her throat, at the thought that Geryon might just *get away with it*. That if she hadn't seen those images, she might have come back none the wiser, and lived out her time as an apprentice in the house of the man who'd done more to hurt her than anyone still alive.

And now that she knew, she couldn't do nothing. She *couldn't*. The anger would build inside her, on and on, forever, until it poisoned her. Every time she saw Geryon, she would return to those images, to the wash of electric fire sweeping down on the *Gideon*. *How can I do* nothing?

He has to answer for it. Somehow, some way, he has to answer.

She could feel her father's eyes on her. It felt like if she turned her head, she'd see his face, frowning in disapproval. *He wouldn't like this.*

Alice sat, deep in thought, for a long time. As the orange light faded to crimson, and then finally to darkness, she realized she'd made her decision.

Her father wouldn't like it. But her father was dead. And she would have her revenge.

END

ACKNOWLEDGMENTS:

My deepest gratitude to the usual suspects:

To Seth Fishman, my agent, for being generally awesome. Also to everyone else at The Gernert Company, Will Roberts, Rebecca Gardner, and Andy Kifer, for also being awesome. Caspian Dennis at Abner Stein is awesome on a completely different continent!

To Elisabeth Fracalossi, my long-serving, long-suffering first reader.

To Kathy Dawson, my editor, for her input and also for putting up with my ignorance of the genre I decided to write in. She has done a great deal to educate me. Also Claire Evans, her assistant, for all her hard work.

To Alexander Jansson, for his spectacular covers and artwork.

To all the hardworking people whose care and effort made this book a reality.

Finally, of course, to everyone who read and spread the word about *The Forbidden Library*: readers, booksellers, librarians, and parents. I couldn't do this without you.

About the Author

Django Wexler graduated from Carnegie Mellon University
in Pittsburgh with degrees in creative writing and computer
science, and worked for the university in artificial intelligence
research. He then migrated to Seattle to work for Microsoft,
but eventually discovered that writing fantasy was
a lot more fun.

As well as *The Forbidden Library* and *The Mad Apprentice*,
Django has also written two epic fantasy novels for adults,
The Thousand Names and *The Shadow Throne*. When not
writing he wrangles computers, paints tiny soldiers, and plays
games of all sorts. He lives with two cats, Tomoes and Sakaki,
who generously assisted the writing process by turning part of
one draft into confetti.

Twitter: @DjangoWexler
Facebook: AuthorDjangoWexler

HAVE YOU ENTERED

THE FORBIDDEN LIBRARY?

Dare you join Alice on her quest to find a happy ending?

'Compulsive fantasy with a brave, brilliant heroine'
Metro

ALSO AVAILABLE

*From the imaginations of bestselling authors Holly Black
and Cassandra Clare comes a heart-stopping plunge
into the magical unknown.*

Most people would do anything to get into
the Magisterium and pass the Iron Trial.

Not Callum Hunt.

Call has been told his whole life that he should
never trust a magician. And so he tries his best
to do his worst – but fails at failing.

Now he must enter the Magisterium. It's a place that's both
sensational and sinister. And Call realizes it has dark ties
to his past and a twisty path to his future.

The Iron Trial is just the beginning.
Call's biggest test is still to come . . .

ALSO AVAILABLE

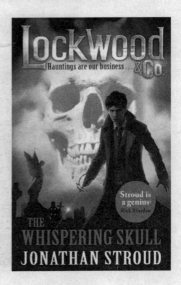

The dead are back to haunt the living.
Evil spirits crowd the streets after dark.
Are you in danger of being ghost-touched?

With ghostly criminal cases on the rise, psychic
Investigations Agents are in demand as never before.
The smallest, most ramshackle – but arguably the best –
of these agencies is Lockwood & Co.

Meet the dashing, scatty Anthony Lockwood;
his loyal, book-loving deputy George Cubbins;
and their newest agent, brave Lucy Carlyle.

Together they must use their Talents to keep you –
and themselves – alive . . .

ALSO AVAILABLE

The first book in John Flanagan's bestselling
Ranger's Apprentice *series*

They have always scared him in the past – the Rangers,
with their dark cloaks and shadowy ways. The villagers believe
the Rangers practise magic that makes them invisible
to ordinary people. And now 15-year-old Will, always small
for his age, has been chosen as a Ranger's apprentice.

What he doesn't yet realize is that the Rangers are the
protectors of the kingdom. Highly trained in the skills
of battle and surveillance, they fight the battles before
the battles reach the people. And as Will is about to learn,
there is a large battle brewing. The exiled Morgarath,
Lord of the Mountains of Rain and Night, is gathering
his forces for an attack on the kingdom. This time,
he will not be denied . . .